Devil's Darning Needle

0410

Linda Holeman

Devil's Darning Needle

The Porcupine's Quill

CANADIAN CATALOGUING IN PUBLICATION DATA

Holeman, Linda
Devil's darning needle

ISBN 0-88984-205-1

I. Title.

PS8565.O6225D48 1999 C813'.54 C99-931163-8
PR9199.3.H5485P76 1999

Canada

Published by The Porcupine's Quill,
68 Main Street, Erin, Ontario NOB 1TO.
Readied for the press by John Metcalf; copy edited by Doris Cowan.
Typeset in Trump, printed on Zephyr Antique laid,
and bound at The Porcupine's Quill Inc.

This is a work of fiction. Any resemblance of characters to persons,
living or dead, is purely coincidental.

Represented in Canada by the Literary Press Group.
Trade orders are available from General Distribution Services.

We acknowledge the support of the Ontario Arts Council,
and the Canada Council for the Arts for our publishing program.
The financial support of the Government of Canada
through the Book Publishing Industry Development Program
is also gratefully acknowledged.

1 2 3 4 • 01 00 99

For my sister, Shannon,
my brothers Randall and Tim,
and in memory of Gregory

Table of Contents

The north wind doth blow,
And we shall have snow,
And what will poor robin do then,
Poor thing?
He'll sit in a barn,
To keep himself warm,
And hide his head under his wing,
Poor thing!

– Anonymous Nursery Rhyme

North Wind

THIS YEAR WAS A HOME YEAR for Christmas. We took turns being shared between the two families, one year with my parents, one year with Wolf's.

We'd always called the farm – Wolf's old home – Home with a capital H, to distinguish it from Alder Avenue, my childhood home. When we were taking Gabriella and Teddie to my parents' we'd say, 'We're going to Alder Avenue,' and they knew they'd be seeing Grandma and Grandpa, here in the city. When we went to Wolf's parents, a tiresome journey of more than 120 miles north on an uninteresting, patchy asphalt highway, we told them we were going 'Home', and they knew they'd be seeing Irmgard and Victor, their Oma and Opa.

This past summer I had suggested to Wolf's parents that they should come into the city and stay with us for Christmas. We could spend the twenty-fifth at Alder Avenue, one big family. Irmgard had looked at me as if I had proposed something outrageous.

'Sleep down there? In the city?' she'd asked, her gnarled hands hovering over Gabriella's glossy braid. Gabriella's hair already reached the small of her back, even though she wasn't quite seven. Now three sections of burnished hair wound over and around Irmgard's arthritic joints.

Before I could reply, Victor had got up from his chair at the kitchen table and headed down the dark hall.

'Sure. You know we have the basement all fixed up now. Wolf finished it last year, remember? There's a nice bedroom down there. And a bathroom. The rec room has a television, and –'

'Wolfgang,' Oma said, looking at her son, 'you know how he is.' Her head tilted in the direction of the hall. 'His stomach.'

Wolf put his ham sandwich onto the plate in front of him and wiped his top lip with the side of his index finger. 'Like Maeve said, Ma, there's a bathroom down there. He could take all the time he likes.'

Another flush echoed down the narrow hall into the kitchen, growing louder as Victor opened the bathroom door.

Irmgard shook her head. 'And there are the turkeys, and Elsa. No. It wouldn't suit.' She made a clucking sound with her tongue to let us know that the conversation was over.

Gabriella gave her head a little jerk and opened her mouth to say something, maybe to urge her Oma to get going on the braid, to complain that it was too tight. To ask what wouldn't suit what. Unlike Teddie, Gabriella always had something to say. But Irmgard tugged gently on the long, shining, half-finished braid.

'Sit still, Gabbie,' she said, her fingers moving again, and Gabriella sat still.

* * *

Wolf never came out and said it, but it was obvious to me that he didn't like coming Home. There was a strange uneasiness between him and his father. I'd asked him a number of times why they couldn't get along, but each time he would shrug, and say typical things like they'd always been at each other's throats, and the old man was too bull-headed and would never change, or that they'd just never seen eye to eye on anything, and never would.

Victor *was* a stiff, uncompromising and somehow bitter person. He'd lived all his life within the same twenty-mile radius, growing up on the next farm with his parents and brother, Frank, who was his elder by ten years. Victor had little schooling; his father hadn't allowed him to go to school past the age of eleven, needing him on the farm. Wolf said that the family had remained pretty well isolated; Frank had been the one to do all the business dealings. Victor's mother died when he was only ten. Wolf says it was probably loneliness and hard work, but no one ever seemed to be able to say for certain what caused her death.

Eventually his father died too, and he and Frank ran the farm on their own. Then Victor met Irmgard, a hired girl on one of the farms in the vicinity, and she and Victor were engaged for seven years, until Victor had saved enough money to buy his own farm – the one on the next property. There had been room for him and Irmgard to stay with Frank, but they hadn't. Frank died an elderly man, still alone.

Neither Victor or Irmgard had any other living relatives. From what Wolf told me, Victor had tried to keep Wolf secluded as he had been in his own childhood, but Wolf had rebelled and left home as soon as he could. Wolf's tiny family was the total opposite of my own. I had three sisters and four brothers, many aunts and uncles and dozens of cousins. We all got together as often as we could.

When Wolf was a young boy, nine or ten, his father had started raising turkeys to supplement their income, butchering and selling them to the surrounding area. He still raised turkeys, although now on a small scale. They were awful things, those turkeys, noisy and seemingly senseless. Their smell was a low, thick vapour over the farm, and the incessant gobbling was as irritating and unrelenting as a keening wind around a loose window frame.

Wolf had to help his father butcher the turkeys each fall, as soon as the weather turned cold. He described it, just once. His father would grab a turkey from the holding pen and hang the flapping bird head down in the mounted, sheet-metal killing cone he'd made. The turkey's head would protrude through the opening at the base of the cone. Wolf's job was to grasp the head, stretching out the neck so his father could give one quick slice to the veins under the throat. While his father was getting the next turkey, Wolf would have to wait one and a half to two minutes while all the turkey's blood, aided by gravity, flowed swiftly out of the veins, before he took it out of the cone. If the blood wasn't completely gone, the skin would have a red, frost-bitten look, lessening the value.

Irmgard had done the scalding and removing of feathers, all by hand, until they could afford an automatic picking machine. Wolf had said the whole procedure was a dismal, distressing task – the flapping, screeching outrage of the turkey as it was hung upside down just before its death, the hot smell of the blood, the carcasses floating in the fifty-five-gallon drum of boiling water. He said he suffered from nightmares every fall, even when he was older. The only good memories he had of the turkeys was the spring arrival of the newly hatched poults, tiny fluffy babies he would cup in both hands.

As Victor grew older he farmed less and less, selling off parcels of his land and renting out other sections; for the past few years he and Irmgard had supported themselves on the turkeys alone. They didn't do the butchering any longer, but sold them live – a truck picked up a load of them before Thanksgiving and then again just before Christmas. The only turkeys killed on the farm now were for Victor and Irmgard's own use.

When we came in the summer the turkey enclosure was full of hundreds of half-grown toms and hens; by Christmas there were less than a dozen.

* * *

I tried to imagine Wolf as a child of five, Teddie's age, playing by himself in the fields or yard or around the draughty house. It made me sad to think of him like that; since I had known him, he hated being alone. He had slid into my own huge family with a kind of quiet relief, as if he were falling into a warm, enveloping pile of eiderdown comforters. There was a look of complete contentment on his face whenever we pushed our way into the crush of adults and children that dominated my parents' house on any holiday gathering.

This Christmas Wolf hadn't wanted to go Home at all. He started complaining in late November, talking about the drive, dragging all the gifts, the frigid upstairs bedrooms, the smell and noise of the turkeys. But I thought we should;

Victor and Irmgard were expecting us. They had no one else. Irmgard had once told me that every second year, the one we didn't come, they went to a pre-Christmas meal at their church in town, and the twenty-fifth passed quietly, a usual day. I didn't like to visualize the two of them like that at Christmas time, even though I wasn't at all close to them. As well, I thought it important for Gabriella and Teddy to have even short snatches of time to get to know their grandparents.

The only other opportunity they had was the one weekend out to the farm every summer. That, and the two or three days every second Christmas was all Wolf would commit to. So I really felt that we shouldn't cancel the planned visit this year, and eventually Wolf came around.

* * *

We'd all been quiet – even Gabriella – on the drive out, late in the afternoon of the twenty-third of December. The road was clear, no snow at all, anywhere. It was the first time I could remember being this close to Christmas without snow. The kids had been anxiously scanning the sky all the way Home, worrying about the snowless effect on Santa and the reindeer. It felt as if there should be snow; it was cold enough. And there was a cold north wind blowing down to meet us as the car nosed its way along the nearly empty highway; I was driving, and could feel the tugging on the steering wheel as the car fought against it.

In winter the farm was usually at its best. A blanket of soft snow softened everything, even giving a trace of beauty to the row of tired jack pines along one side of the barn. The tilting grey fence posts of the huge turkey enclosure would have an almost festive look with tall, jaunty white caps. The snow also helped to deaden the noise of the small tight crowd of turkeys, and the cold killed much of the smell. But this year, with no insulating layer, the farm was a bleak place. As I stepped out of the car the ground was hard, unforgiving under my boots. The empty grey sky was ragged and bleak, as if in mourning. Besides the non-stop grumbling murmur of the turkeys, only one harsh cry of a jay in the pines broke through that stratum of frozen, dead air.

'Cover your nose, quick, Teddie,' Gabriella instructed as they scrambled out of the back seat. 'Don't swallow that smell or it will go into your stomach and make you sick.'

Teddie jammed his mittened hand over his nose and mouth, his eyes wide above the blue wool. He hated the turkeys. Even as a toddler, with Wolf carrying him, he had screamed, high, surreal baby shrieks of panic at the sight of the bobbing, cackling mass behind the boarded compound. Last summer he wouldn't even go out of the house unless Wolf or I were with him.

I looked at Wolf, watched him lifting bags out of the trunk to see if the change, the one that always came over him when he was Home, had begun. It made him silent, edgy, sharp with the kids. I was sorry for his mother to see him like that. I tried to explain, more than once, that Wolf was really a good dad; that he spent a lot of time with both kids, and had more patience than I did. But she would just listen and nod, her small brown eyes following her son around the kitchen with what looked to me to be a sorry resignation.

* * *

The next day, Irmgard and I helped the kids decorate the little spruce Victor had cut out in the bush. We were planning to have our Christmas meal and open our gifts that evening, in Victor and Irmgard's traditional German way. While we were getting the tree done, Wolf went out with his father to help him feed the turkeys, and when they came in for lunch they were silent, neither meeting anyone's eyes. I encouraged the children's chatter at the table, feeling as if the heaviness of the frigid outside atmosphere had somehow leached into the kitchen with the arrival of Victor and Wolf.

After lunch we took the kids out to the barn. Gabriella wanted to pat Elsa, the cow Victor and Irmgard kept for milk. Gabriella remembered her from the previous years; last summer she had even managed to milk Elsa, squeezing a few jets of frothing milk into the tin pail. We entered the cavernous space, empty but for the old brown-and-white cow. The only apparent warmth came from the humid, green-smelling snuffles of air she blew out of her massive nostrils as she absently chewed. Gabriella ignored her, running to an empty wooden trough on legs that stood against one wall.

'Hey, this looks like the manger. The one for the baby Jesus.' She picked up an armload of loose straw and threw it into the trough. 'Come here, Teddie, look.'

Teddie glanced around him, then went over. Gabriella piled more straw into the big wooden trough. Watching her, Teddie began to sing, his voice thin and reedy, the barn echoing his words.

'*Away in a manger, no crib for a bed,*' he sang.

Gabriella ignored him, intent on her work. I smiled and glanced up at Wolf, wanting to share this picture with him, our two children, so different – one industrious and practical, the other dreamy and sensitive. But Wolf was watching the scene with an unreadable expression on his face, and didn't return my look. I leaned my head against his shoulder, but still he didn't move.

Teddie continued to sing.

'*The cattle are lowing,*

the baby awakes,

but little Lord Jesus.' He hesitated.

'*But little Lord Jesus* ... what's the next line?'

Wolf answered. 'No crying He makes.'

'Oh yeah, *no crying He makes,*' Teddie repeated, half singing, half talking. 'Come and see, Mom, Dad. Gabriella's making a manger.'

I went over to look at the little bed Gabriella was patting into place. But Wolf stayed where he was.

'You get in, Teddie,' Gabriella said, when she had smoothed the straw down in the centre, and made an extra hump for a pillow at one end. 'Get in the manger. Lie down in the straw, and you can be the baby Jesus.'

'Okay,' Teddie said, and put one foot up on the side of the trough.

'*NO*!' Wolf said.

We all turned and looked at him.

'Get away from there. Get away!' Wolf strode over to Teddie and grabbed him by the arm. 'You'll get all dirty.'

'It's all right, Wolf,' I said. 'It's only –'

'*I said no*!'

'Daddy,' Teddie whined, pulling at Wolf's fingers, wrapped completely around his small upper arm.

Gabriella had already tired of the game. 'Let's go see Elsa, Teddie.' She left the three of us and marched over to the stall where the cow stood watching us.

I saw Wolf's hand on Teddie's arm, the tightness of his grip, and reached out and touched it. 'Wolf?'

He looked at me, then down at Teddie, dropping the boy's arm as it if had burned him. He jammed his hands into his pockets and turned away, toward his daughter, and the cow.

* * *

'Hi, Elsa. Hi, moo cow,' Gabriella said. She had climbed onto a narrow strip of wood on the bottom of the stall gate, so she could reach up to the cow. 'Why is her name Elsa?'

'I don't know,' I answered. 'I guess Oma and Opa liked that name.'

'Last summer Oma said she gave the most milk of any cow she ever knew. Come on, Teddie. Come and see Elsa. Pat her.'

Teddie shook his head. I put my arm around his shoulders.

Gabriella frowned at her brother. 'She won't hurt you, Teddie. Don't be such a baby. Come see.' She stroked the animal's broad nose. Its wide, square teeth chewed sideways, jaw swivelling.

'I don't like her,' Teddie said. 'I like her better than the turkeys, but I still don't like her.'

Wolf finally left the manger, and came toward Teddie. He squatted in front of him. 'Why not? Why don't you like the cow?'

Teddie shrugged, studying his father's face. His own small features were guarded, closed. Then he put his head back and looked up at the high, dusty ceiling of the barn. I followed his gaze. Fingers of light came in through cracks in the ceiling, and dusty particles floated in the shafts of brighter air.

'I don't know,' he said. 'I don't like this place, either. It's too big. And it smells. It's scary.'

Wolf stayed on his haunches in front of Teddie. 'I used to be scared, too.'

I didn't believe him. Wolf often said things to allay Teddie's fears, agreed with him about frightening things, telling him that when he was a little boy he too had felt that way. Although it wasn't totally honest, it worked. It was a way of helping Teddie through some of his worries.

'Of this barn?' Teddie asked.

Wolf reached out and put his hand on the splintered wood of the wall beside him, as if to steady himself, then straightened his knees and stood up. 'No. Not this barn. Another one.'

'Which one?'

Not looking at Teddie, Wolf said, 'I had to go to my uncle's farm every Saturday, starting when I was a little older than you. My Uncle Frank's. To take him baking Oma did for him, and to help him with some of the chores. And I didn't like his barn. He had a whole herd of cows. The barn was really cold and dark. And dirty. Scary.'

It sounded as if it could be true. But Wolf had never told me anything about his uncle, only that he had died the year Wolf left home. He said his father and uncle had stopped speaking to each other before Wolf was even born, and they hadn't seen each other for years and years. So why would he make Wolf go and help him?

Teddie reached out and ran his fingertip along the open zipper of Wolf's jacket. 'What chores did you have to do there?'

Wolf picked a piece of straw out of Teddie's light hair. I knew, now, from the dark look on Wolf's face, that this wasn't a made-up story. 'All kinds of things. Uncle Frank had lots of animals, besides the cows. A couple of horses. Pigs, ducks. A goat.'

'Turkeys?'

Wolf shook his head. 'Sometimes I had to feed all the animals. Shovel out the manure.'

'What's manure?'

'Poop,' Gabriella called, jumping down from the gate. 'It's cow poop. Mrs Oleska told us that when we went on our field trip to that farm last year.'

'Ewwww,' Teddie said, pinching his nose with his fingers. 'Shovelling cow poop.' He gave a small giggle, and moved away from Wolf.

Gabriella joined in, her laughter loud and bold. 'Poop,' she said, 'poop.' They both laughed harder and harder, and then Gabriella started chasing Teddie up and down the long open corridor between the empty stalls, pretending she had a handful of manure. Their high, uninhibited whoops of joy soared up to the ceiling where they thinned and finally faded against the rigid, supporting beams of the roof.

* * *

When Teddie started complaining about being cold, Wolf and I took him back to the house. The wind had died down overnight, but I noticed, as we made our way back to the house, that it had started again. It had a sharp, damp bite. Still, Gabriella wanted to stay out in the yard, so we left her, swinging on the length of knotted rope Victor had tied to a tree branch on our visit out two summers ago. Every so often she yelled 'Be quiet!' at the turkeys, or made throaty, mocking sounds at the enclosure.

Victor was sitting at one end of the table, smoking his pipe. A bottle of Jim Beam was in front of him, along with a small empty glass and a heavy green ceramic ashtray. Irmgard was washing a plucked turkey in the sink. Its flesh was bluish, pimply and chilled-looking.

Teddy scrambled onto the chair behind the table, close to the wall, while Wolf got out a glass and sat across from his father.

'What do you want me to do, Irmgard?'

The woman nodded toward a plastic bag of dry heels of bread. 'You can tear that up, and start cooking it. The onions are chopped, there, and you can put in the sage and salt and pepper. I want to get this stuffed and in the oven right away, so we can eat by,' she glanced at the clock, 'by seven.' She slapped the bird, a wet smack. 'This one should take about five hours.'

I washed my hands and stood beside her at the counter, pulling the bread apart and dropping it into the big bowl she handed to me. I hoped she wouldn't ask me to put the stuffing into the turkey. The chickens and turkeys I stuffed in my own kitchen were antiseptic, neutral in their hard plastic shrouds, bought from the meat cooler at Safeway. Impersonal, with no more imagined life than the slabs of red beef or the round pork roasts that shared space with them in the cooler. But I knew that this big turkey, the one Irmgard was casually subjecting to jets of icy water, picking at tiny bits of embedded feather shafts, had been alive the day before. It had been pecking its way around its home, warmed by the bodies of the other turkeys, possibly even communicating in some secret, gobbling way. And now it sat, headless, lifeless, in the stainless steel of the sink. The idea of placing my hand into that cold, dark interior filled me with a sudden unexpected melancholy.

I heard the clink of glass and the gurgling sound of pouring liquid. Then the *phht phht* of Victor and his pipe.

'Would you like me to make you some cocoa, Teddie?' Irmgard asked.

'Yes, Oma,' Teddie answered. I knew he would sit there, at the table, just watching and listening. He'd always been that way, even as a toddler. Not like Gabriella, who needed to move and jump and touch and talk. I had once even asked the pediatrician if he thought it all right, the way Teddie was so quiet and undemanding.

'Some children are lively, some aren't,' the doctor reassured me. 'Some accept the way things are, content to not change anything, but to internalize. Take things in slowly, turn them around and examine them, in here.' He'd tapped the side of his head. 'And some think it's their job to change everything around them, to stir things up. That's how *they* deal with their lives.' He'd smiled at Gabriella, then a very busy three-year-old.

'So this year is your small Christmas, here with us,' Irmgard said, taking down a tin canister of cocoa from the cupboard over her head. I listened for anything negative in the words or tone, but there was nothing.

'It's nice to have change,' I said. 'And remember, like I said before, any time you want a bigger and noisier Christmas, come and stay with us.'

'We like it this way,' Irmgard said. 'We're too old for change.' She set a pot on the stove.

'Don't you get lonely?' Teddie asked. 'Just you and Opa?' He leaned back so that the front two legs of the chair tipped off the floor. The back of the chair hit the wall behind him.

'Oh, no,' Irmgard answered, quickly. 'Do we, Opa?' The fridge door opened and then slammed as she took out the milk.

Victor grunted around his pipe stem.

Teddie lowered the front legs of his chair, then rocked them back again. 'Did you get lonely when you were a little boy, Daddy? Were you lonely, over in that scary barn?'

I heard the back of the chair hit the wall two more times.

'Teddie,' Oma said. 'Stop rocking your chair. You'll tip over.'

'Listen to Oma, Teddie,' I said, my hands still busy with the bread.

But Teddie tipped his chair back again. I turned around, surprised.

'Where's that Uncle Frank now, Daddy?'

I saw the look that passed over Wolf's face.

'Pah!' Opa said, his lips twisting. 'The old bugger. He's down below, where he belongs.'

'Where below?' Teddie asked. He rocked the front two legs of his chair off the wooden floor again, leaning back. Oma didn't repeat her warning. 'Why is he an old bugger, Opa?'

When his grandfather didn't answer, he looked back at Wolf. 'That's a bad word, bugger. Is he a bugger because he made you do that work? Where you were scared of the barn?'

The room grew very still. Don't, Teddie, I said in my head. Something about the whole episode out in Victor's barn, Wolf barking at Teddie about the straw, and his strange, tiny bit of the never-before-told story had somehow unnerved me. Don't keep asking, I told Teddie, silently. Stop now.

And as if he had heard my inner voice, wanted to respond to the message I was sending him, Teddie gave his chair one final hard push, and the back legs slipped forward and the chair tipped under the table, hitting the uncarpeted floor with a loud crack at the same time the back of Teddie's head bounced against the floorboards with a heavy, dull thud.

I hurried over to him, Irmgard following me. Victor half rose from his chair, then sat back down. Only Wolf stayed where he was, unmoving except for his eyes, looking at Teddie with a kind of calm wonder.

'See?' Irmgard cried as I pulled Teddie out from under the table. 'See, Teddie? I told you. Is he hurt, Maeve?' She came over to where I was kneeling, cradling Teddie. He wasn't crying, but his lips had lost their colour, and suddenly his cheekbones were very visible in his narrow face.

'Let me see, honey,' I said, putting my hand under the back of his head.

'Ow,' Teddie whimpered.

'You'll have a goose egg, that's for sure,' I said, helping him up, feeling his shoulder blades, small sharp wings under the warm fleece of his sweatshirt. 'You're being so brave,' I said, as he got to his feet and Irmgard pulled the chair upright.

He shrugged, his bottom lip beginning to tremble, his eyes sliding in his father's direction.

'Isn't he being brave, Wolf?'

Victor got up again, knocking his pipe against the edge of the ashtray. As he knocked, a small dark pyramid of tobacco began to form on the green bottom. 'He just bumped his head. You shouldn't tell him he's brave for nothing.' He picked up a short sharp piece of metal, a tiny sword-shaped implement, and dug into the pipe bowl. More dottle spilled out. 'He didn't listen to his grandmother, and he fell over and bumped his head. He could have broken the chair. He should be punished, not praised.'

'Punished?' His chair pushing back with a screech, Wolf stood. '*Punished*?'

'Wolfgang –' Irmgard started, but Wolf ignored her.

'He's five years old, for Chrissakes.' Wolf's voice was far too loud; something was more wrong than the fact that Teddie had fallen.

Irmgard looked at me, her eyes slightly unfocused. Her shoulders came up a fraction of an inch, and she looked back at Wolf as he walked toward his father.

Wolf stood in front of Victor, at least four inches taller than the old man. 'A kid falls over, and you think he should be punished? But then that's typical, isn't it, Pop? Typical of you, and your way of thinking. Of the way of your whole damn family.' He was shouting now.

Teddie pressed his face against my stomach. I could feel his warm breath through the thin wool of my sweater and right through my jeans.

'Couldn't you ever find anything to say, any kind word, to a kid, especially when he's hurt? What would it have taken you to give him one shred of comfort? Couldn't you ever, for once, realize you should have done something? You should have helped? What kind of a father were you? What kind?'

Victor tossed the metal scraper onto the table and straightened his shoulders. 'I was a good father to you. I never laid a hand on you. And I was proud, proud of you, and you know it.'

A bitter look crossed Wolf's face. 'Proud of me? Yeah. I remember the one time you were proud of me. And what I had to do for you to give me that pat on the shoulder, that nod. I had to practically kill Uncle Frank. Isn't that right? Isn't that right, Pop? And I had to do it for you, because you were too fucking afraid of him.'

I covered Teddie's ears with my hands. His head, hot, was motionless, but alert, listening beneath my palms.

Victor drew back as if Wolf had struck him. His breath hissed out between his front teeth.

'You think I didn't know?' Wolf asked, his voice quieter. 'You think I didn't figure it out? I was only thirteen, but Christ! I knew what must have happened to you. The same thing that was happening to me at the hands of good old Uncle Frank. Your big brother. But you wouldn't help me, would you? And I knew I could never come crying to you about it, could I? I wasn't allowed to cry about anything. Remember? You sent me there, and kept sending me there, waiting for me to stand up for myself, waiting for me to prove that I was more of a man than you ever were. And the day I finally did it, finally showed him that he couldn't do whatever he wanted, the day I took care of business for myself – and for you – that was the one and only time you made me feel that I'd done something right.'

Victor reached behind, feeling for his chair. He lowered himself into it, the now empty pipe still in his hand. The only sound in the kitchen was the ticking of the stove timer. I could feel a round wet spot in my sweater where Teddie's open mouth was still pressed. I stroked his hair, running my fingertips along the delicate scallop of his ear.

Wolf looked at his father for another few seconds, then around the room, as if he'd never seen it before. Finally his eyes settled on me, on Teddie. 'We're leaving,' he said. 'I'm going out to start the car. I'll get Gabriella, and be in to help you pack everything up in a minute.'

Without waiting to put on his jacket, he grabbed the keys off the counter and went out to the yard. The door slammed behind him, and a furious whoosh of air swirled across the kitchen floor.

'But the turkey,' Irmgard said, to no one in particular.

* * *

When we got into the car, Gabriella was crying. 'But I want to stay here. What if Santa gets mixed up now? He thinks we're at Oma and Opa's. Why do we have to go?'

I tried to shush her, glancing at Teddie. He had two dark red spots on his cheeks. As soon as Wolf pulled the car out onto the main road, Teddie called, from the back seat,

'I want to see that barn, Daddy. Are you still scared of it?'

Wolf sighed. 'No. No, Teddy, I'm not.'

'Where is it?'

Wolf turned up the heater. A steady stream of warm air blew into my face. 'It burned down.'

'Why?'

'I don't know. After Uncle Frank died another family bought his farm. Oma said that the barn burned down a few years ago – not the house, just the barn. The family moved away, and no one else has touched the farm since.'

'So the barn's gone?'

'I think so, most of it, anyway. Your Oma said there's still the charred skeleton of it, just a lot of black wood.'

'Can we go and look at it?'

Wolf slowed the car, eventually coming to a stop. We sat in the grey afternoon for maybe thirty seconds, until Gabriella stopped sniffing and called, 'What are we doing?'

Wolf put the car in reverse and made a U-turn in the middle of the road, so that we were facing north again.

'Are we going back to Oma and Opa's?' Gabriella asked.

Wolf drove, past his parents' place, until he came to a side road. 'It's a ways down this road. A mile or so. It's farther by road than across the fields. I always went across the fields.'

Teddie settled back against the seat, his head turned toward the window. Gabriella bounced her stuffed elephant up and down on her lap. After two minutes Teddie leaned forward.

'Did we miss it? Did we miss the barn?'

'No. No, it's up ahead. Just there, around the next bend.'

As the car started to follow the curve of the road, the gentle shift to the left, something hit the windshield. Then again. A wet plop.

'Rain,' Wolf murmured.

'No,' I said. 'Not rain. Wolf, maybe you should turn on the lights. It's dark, for so early in the day.'

Wolf flicked on the headlights. The snowflakes suddenly came alive, dancing in front of the two yellow beams.

'Gabriella, Teddie,' I said. 'It's starting to snow. We'll have snow for Christmas, after all.'

I turned to look over my left shoulder, and in that brief instant, just before my eyes focused on the children's faces, they passed over Wolf's profile. It was pale in the faint green gleam of the lit dashboard, and I saw that his lips were slightly parted, the whole right side of his face tense, pulled forward in concentration. He stared ahead, far beyond the quiet drift of snowflakes in the soft glow of the headlights, so as not to miss it, not to miss the blackened remains of the old barn, leaning to the south, still leaning, even in its ruined state, cowering from the north wind.

For nothing can be sole or whole
that has not been rent.

– William Butler Yeats
Words for Music, Perhaps, 1932

Devil's Darning Needle

KRISTEN STUDIES THE GRASS alongside the gravel road. She slaps at a mosquito on her neck, and watches the dragonflies flitting in and out of the thick grass sprouting at the sides of the road. The dragonflies come in singles and pairs; when there are two, one appears to be flying just over the tail of the other. Kristen wonders if one is teaching the other something, directing it somewhere. Or whether one is chasing the other away from something, territory, or food, or a prospective mate. Or whether they are mating, although they don't seem to be actually touching one another. But then who knows, she asks herself, if they really have to touch when they mate. She doesn't know much about dragonflies, except that her grandmother called them darning needles – no, her actual name for the insect was a devil's darning needle.

Kristen never understood why her grandmother associated such beautiful creatures with the Devil. She remembered a girl down the street she played with one summer who would often capture a resting dragonfly and put it against her shirt. The insect would cling there, seemingly unperturbed, a living, glistening brooch. Once the girl had lifted one off her own shirt and deposited onto the front of Kristen's T-shirt. Fascinated with the beautiful, harmless creature, Kristen looked down at it, wondered what made it stay, so trusting, against the colourful cotton stripes. Was it listening to the rhythmic whisper of her heart, or enjoying the warmth radiating from her body on that hot day? She watched it for about ten minutes, all the while walking in slow circles around her grassy front yard. And then, as if called, the dragonfly serenely moved its wings and rose up into the summer sky, first swooping once around Kristen as if bidding her farewell.

Another small green van is making its way down the narrow lane, brakes groaning. She and Brent had come in the first van. There was a second that expelled its group of five young men, all speaking loudly. Australian accents. This is the third van. It stops; the door opens and an elderly woman steps down, squinting in the haze of the August morning. She turns around and puts her hand out, up, into the open door of the van. A man, his head lowered in the doorway, reaches for her offered hand.

'Careful, Lawrence,' the woman says.

The man, thin to the point of gauntness, jumps down with both feet, jumps too hard on long, brilliantly white running shoes, creating a small grey cloud of dust. He smiles at the dust he created, at the woman. A much older man follows him, putting each foot down precisely on the metal running board, then on the ground. They stand in a tight triangle in front of the van; the tall, skeletal man flanked by the two shorter, older people. Their arms press against each other, as if they are used to standing like this, tight, holding each other up. They look at the water, and at the rafts on the pebbly shore. They look at Kristen and Brent. Kristen smiles, and then she looks back at the coarse grass and the dragonflies.

'Jeez. Why'd they bring a guy like that along?' Brent says.

Kristen keeps smiling, but says, her lips barely moving, 'Shut up, Brent.'

'They can't hear me.'

Kristen's voice is low. 'Why shouldn't they bring him?'

Brent looks over at her. 'Come ON, Kristen. This is a rafting excursion. Not some kind of field trip.'

'It's none of your business, Brent.' Kristen keeps her voice low, controlled. 'None of your business who belongs here and who doesn't.' She keeps looking at him, but thinks, Damn, I told myself I wouldn't do this, wouldn't start anything. Would just shut up, for these two weeks, and watch, and listen. Listen to Brent, listen to my own feelings. And I'm doing it already.

Brent stares into her eyes. There is something there. Something Kristen doesn't recognize. 'We're here, aren't we, Kristen? I told you I didn't want to do this rafting thing.'

'And I told YOU that I didn't want to come down here, to Wyoming, of all places. So now that we're here, I should get to pick at least ONE thing that I want to do.'

Brent's eyes drop away, and Kristen feels a small, thin note of triumph clang in her head. She immediately tries to push it away. She agreed to come here, to Wyoming, to stay at a small dude ranch and ride horses and look at the stars at night and try to pull together the torn edges of the remains of what she and Brent once had.

It started so strongly, almost three years ago. Now there seemed to only be strings of frayed emotions, threads of half-finished conversations. Everything felt undone, pulling apart. And it seemed that all she could do was watch, pick on him, wait for him to show her something that would remind her how much she loved him, how much she wanted them to stay together. And she couldn't see how a holiday would help any of that. She'd told him that, right from the start.

'I don't think so, Brent,' she'd said, in early June, looking out the third-floor apartment windows to the roofs of the cars parked along the street.

'Well, I do. I think we should,' Brent had said. 'We've both been working too hard. And you haven't taken a vacation for about two years.'

Kristen shrugged, then turned to face Brent. He was sitting on the couch, with Lizzie in his lap. Lizzie's eyes were yellow slits of pleasure, and her prim cat mouth lengthened each time Brent's hand pushed down between her ears in firm, hard strokes that ran the length of her sleek black body.

Brent didn't look up as he spoke. 'Maybe we've just forgotten to have fun together. We used to have so much fun. It's like we've let everything slide. Sometimes it's too easy to just let go. Just let go,' he repeated, softer.

'I know.' Kristen turned back to the baked gleam of the car roofs. 'But I don't think a holiday is going to make things better. It's like the couple who say they should have a baby to strengthen their relationship. Everything just falls apart even more, with the added stress.'

There is a small snuffle from the couch, a blowing-out of air. Kristen isn't sure if it's Brent or Lizzie. 'You could use a holiday. Just some time alone together. I can take my holidays in August. Could you swing it?'

'And you really think a week away, or even two, would make any difference?' Kristen said to her reflection in the window. 'Can patch up all the holes?'

There is silence in the apartment except for the shushing of the air conditioner.

'We have to start somewhere,' Brent finally answers, 'if we want to hold on to this thing. Keep it together.'

At the tone of his voice, Kristen felt her first surge of hope. His voice had been sad, quiet, none of his usual breezy, confident charm. Kristen felt he was, in the only way he could, admitting it, finally letting her see that he was scared, too. It was all she could do to keep herself from going over to him and putting her arms around him.

'Well, okay, if you really want to,' was what she had said.

* * *

'All right, people, listen up,' a voice calls from near the water. Kristen looks over at the man standing in one of the rafts, wearing a T-shirt that says I GOT SLOSHED AT THE GRAND TETONS!! The ten people on shore all look at him.

'Name's Rick. You can call me Rick, Richard, Ricardo, or the Rich Man.' He waits for the tiny ripple of polite laughter. 'I'm one of your oarsman on this particular run.' He raises a Styrofoam cup to his lips and takes a quick slurp.

'Just black coffee, folks,' he says, one corner of his lip rising in the parody of a smile. Kristen wonders why anyone would think any different, at eight in the morning. 'To get you safely back here I'm gonna need all six of my senses in the next few hours.' He pauses again.

Kristen doesn't even bother to smile. Even though Rick is probably the same age as her and Brent, or maybe even younger, in his early twenties, he reminds her of some old, arrogant comedian, Bob Hope maybe, or George Burns. One of those ancient guys who always waited for the laughter before heading into his next line.

'Because these are the smaller rafts,' he continues, gesturing to the row behind him, 'we can't have more than six bodies per raft. I'll take you guys, here,' he says, making a circle in the air with his hand, drawing in Brent and Kristen and the three from the last van. 'And my buddy Hank over there,' his hand stops at an equally young, but better-looking man standing in another raft, 'will take you people.' He draws another vague circle in the direction of the group of five men on the pebble-strewn shore, then pulls a package of cigarettes out of the back pocket of his cut-offs, and puts a cigarette into the side of his mouth.

'One for the road,' he says, the other half of his mouth smiling this time. He lights the cigarette with a practised flick of the lighter he took out of the package. 'I'll finish this off before we leave. Come on, come on down closer.' He motions his group towards him, the cigarette bobbing from his lip, one eye closed as smoke curls upward.

'My group, right here. Everyone grab a life jacket.' He rolls the cigarette package up in his T-shirt sleeve.

'Great,' Brent murmurs into the hair covering Kristen's left ear as they start to walk towards the raft. 'We get stuck with James Dean and the Addams Family.'

Kristen gets a sudden whiff of drying rubber. She looks out at the grey expanse of water, at the low, early morning mist hanging dully over the bushy shoreline. She forces herself to think about the water, about the dragonflies, so she won't say anything to Brent, won't make things worse.

Brent steps into the raft, then turns and takes the top of Kristen's arm. She climbs in, stepping between lifeless torsos, the stained life jackets lying in the bottom of the raft. She picks up a yellow one. As she slips her bare arms through the armholes, the musty odour rises up, into her nostrils. The jacket is damp and chills her skin, right through her tank top. She feels her breasts shrivel.

As the old man and woman help the younger man over the

raft's high sides, Kristen fusses with the plastic buckles of her life jacket, looking down. She wishes she hadn't witnessed the man's uncoordinated legs and feet, his exaggerated, over-stepping into the raft, as if he were blindfolded, walking out into the unknown.

'Let's find a life jacket for you, Lawrence,' she hears the woman say. 'Father, hand me that orange one. Orange is Lawrence's favourite colour.'

Kristen sits down on the round, hard edge of the raft, beside Brent. Rick has traded places with them, is standing on the shore, talking to Hank. Kristen watches as he gestures toward the raft, but can't hear what he's saying. He looks at the group in his raft, his eyes meeting Kristen's for a second. He turns his back.

'Well,' she hears the other woman say, 'maybe we should introduce ourselves.'

Kristen looks at her. The woman's face is seamed with fine lines, and her hair is short, the white curls tightly permed. Her back is slightly humped under her shapeless short-sleeved shirt; her arms are thick, as are the thighs emerging from the long, baggy legs of wrinkled pink shorts. Her legs, from the ankle to where they disappear into the shorts, are painful to look at, covered with thick ropes and knots of purple and maroon and navy.

'I'm Sophie, and that there's Gerald, my husband.' She fans her fingers in the direction of the older man, also in shorts. His are tan-coloured, and neatly pressed. A camera, old and boxy, hangs around his neck on a worn leather strap.

The old man touches the brim of his fishing hat, covered with feathered lures and plastic badges. His long thin legs, unlike Sophie's, are smooth, hairless, with only pale blue shadows of veins. His cheeks are pink and as smooth as his legs. His eyebrows seem to have taken on the job of making up for all the missing body hair; they're huge and thick and sprout wildly, meeting over the bridge of his nose and beetling, wide and furry, down beside his eyes.

'Hello,' Kristen says, smiling. From the corner of her eye

she sees Brent's nod. 'I'm Kristen.' She turns to Brent, but he's looking down at his feet. Kristen follows his gaze, and sees that the toes of his beat-up Timberlakes are in a small pool of water. As she wonders if Brent will speak, say hello, Sophie continues.

'And this is our son, Lawrence,' she says, closing the open second of silence easily, as if she is used to moments of silence. She reaches up to let her hand rest lightly on the back of the padded life jacket on the tall man still standing beside her.

Kristen looks at the woman's hand, the arthritic knuckles, the way the slightly curled fingers touch the life jacket softly, almost tenderly. Kristen suddenly realizes she's staring, that something is expected of her, and raises her eyes to the younger man's face.

'Hi, Lawrence,' she says.

'Kristen,' Lawrence says, his voice deep. Kristen feels a start of surprise; she thought that if this man spoke at all, his voice would be high. Lawrence holds out his hand, again surprising Kristen, and she reaches up and puts her hand in his. Lawrence's fingers close around hers. His hand is big, and dry and warm, the clasp like that of some soft material, worn wool, or possibly old leather. He begins pumping, so hard that Kristen's arm moves up and down from the shoulder; Lawrence pumps her hand as if trying to prime a long-empty well.

'Kristen, Kristen, Kristen,' he says, rocking back and forth over their joined hands.

'All right, Lawrence,' Gerald says, touching Lawrence's arm. Lawrence opens his fingers so quickly that Kristen's hand is left hanging in mid-air. She reaches over, and like Gerald did to Lawrence, touches Brent's arm. 'This is Brent,' she says, too loudly. 'Brent,' she repeats, softer this time.

Lawrence thrusts his hand forward again. 'Brent,' he says, in the same dignified tone. 'Brent, Br– ' he stops as Brent grabs his hand and gives it one hard, quick shake, like he was closing a business deal with one of his real estate clients. He pulls his hand away before Lawrence has a chance to get a grip. Kristen sees that Brent's face is pale under his tan.

Lawrence looks at Sophie. She smiles and nods, and Lawrence smiles back at her. Then Sophie sits down on the edge of the raft, across from Kristen and Brent, and pats the rubber beside her. Lawrence sits, and looks up at Gerald. Slowly the older man lowers himself on the other side of Lawrence, his knees wide apart. He places his long, slender fingers on top of his knees, as if holding them in place.

'Okay, let's get ready to move out,' Rick says, walking toward the raft. He stops and surveys his crew, blows one perfect smoke ring, then flicks the glowing cigarette onto the wet stones. He tosses his Styrofoam cup into the bottom of the raft, where it rolls from side to side. Kristen sees that the rim is nibbled; there are half-moon thumbnail prints in neat, systematic rows around the bottom of the cup.

Rick fills his lungs with air. 'You all ready to ROCK AND ROLL?' In spite of the words, Rick's tone lacks enthusiasm. Kristen wonders if he is sick of doing this, twice a day, all summer, or just disappointed in the five of them.

'Rock and roll, rock and roll,' Lawrence echoes. Rick grins at him.

'Here we go, then. Wagons ho-o,' Rick announces. He gives the raft a hard push, and leaps in just before his black-and-white sneakers touch the water.

'A-lowwww-HA!' Lawrence says, his voice rising to a shout on the last syllable. Sophie pats the pointed bone of his blue-jean-covered knee.

'Is there anything, you know, really dangerous?' Kristen calls to Rick.

'Nah,' Rick says. 'A few bumps. Just fun. I'll let you know when to hold on. This stretch of the Snake River has medium rapids. We don't take kids under twelve, but there's really nothing to worry about. As long as you hold on when I tell you.'

Kristen thinks of the release form she and Brent signed when they paid for the ride at the Water Adventure kiosk on a corner of the street in Jackson Hole.

'What's this shit?' Brent had said, reading the first few lines. 'What does this mean, relinquishing all responsibility? Of course they're responsible if something happens. I'm not signing this.' He'd put the form back on the counter.

'Don't be stupid,' Kristen said. 'You have to sign these for everything. We'll probably even have one for the horseback riding tomorrow. Just sign it.' She'd scribbled her name on hers, then, after five or six seconds, grabbed Brent's and wrote his name on it, shoving the papers and her Visa card back at the young girl in the kiosk.

She'd been surprised when Brent hadn't said anything more about it.

* * *

Rick sits down on one end of the raft and starts to row. He waves to Hank, who is a few hundred metres ahead, and nods.

'This is fun, isn't it, Father?' Sophie says. Not waiting for an answer, she adds, 'But the river is a little different than that last one. Wider. More brush on the sides. Maybe we'll see some deer. Deer, Lawrence.'

'You've rafted before?' Kristen asks.

'Yup,' Gerald answers. 'Rafting, fishing, you name it, if it's on or in water. And we've seen a lot of water – all over the U.S. of A. Everything from cruises up to Alaska to snorkelling in Hawaii. Lawrence here, well, he's an excellent swimmer – loves the water. Likes to try something new every year,' he adds.

'Each winter we plan our summer vacation,' Sophie says. 'We've been to twenty-seven states, a different state each summer since Lawrence learned to walk.' She looks at her son. 'Like Father said, our boy's favourite holidays are around water.'

Kristen wonders how Sophie and Gerald know this. If they discuss these planned holidays with Lawrence, if he says he likes water. If he has really said that orange is his favourite colour.

'She's quiet today,' Rick says, looking out at the water as he pulls on the oars. 'All the fight knocked out of her by yesterday's storm.'

Kristen tilts her head back and looks at the sky. It's dishwater grey, flat and dull as the river. She glances at Brent, but his face is as closed as the sky, the water. Nothing moves anywhere, except for the smooth slide of the oars, the empty cup rolling in the bottom of the raft, the rhythmic rocking of Lawrence's close-cropped head.

After a while Rick starts talking again, breaking the stillness, something about how long he's been riding the Snake, pointing out interesting-shaped rocks along the sides of the river, and telling them where to watch for wildlife. They go over a few minor ripples of rapids, and each time, Lawrence shouts, 'Here we go!'

* * *

After an hour they stop. The sun is deciding whether it will bother to tear through the heavy pewter curtain, only occasionally allowing a tiny, reluctant sliver of light to slip out. When it does, it reflects upward from the water, and lights the underside of the passengers' faces. Kristen hears a distant thrum, and thinks of Lizzie and her purring, or the working of a giant beehive.

'Gonna take a little break here, folks,' Rick says. He pulls an insulated bag out from under a tarp in the corner of the raft. 'Anyone want a drink?' he asks, reaching into the bag. 'Coke and Dr Pepper today.' He takes out a few cans and passes them around. Kristen's burgundy can is wet and slippery.

'What you're hearing is one of the bigger sets of rapids, downriver,' Rick says.

'Aren't you having your drink?' Kristen asks Brent, taking a sip of the too-sweet Dr Pepper.

He shakes his head. Kristen notices that his lips are curiously thin, and straight. He looks even more pale. He seems angry.

It's because of Lawrence, Kristen thinks. Because of

Lawrence and Sophie and Gerald. He doesn't like them, because they're not perfect. No, she decides, he's angry with me. Because I wanted to do this, and he didn't.

'Okay,' Rick says, when they've finished their drinks and he's collected the empty cans and stored them back in the cooler, 'get ready. We're coming up to the rapids. Like I said, nothing to worry about. We'll lift and drop, lift and drop. It'll rattle your insides, but no worse than some crazy ride at an amusement park. So get comfortable, and make sure you hang on to the rope, here. Like this.' He sits on the floor and leans back, stretching both arms along the top of the raft, his hands wrapping around the thick yellow nylon rope that's threaded through big rubber loops. The rope runs around the whole top of the raft.

'That's it. Just hold on. It's safer down here – you won't get bounced off. And you won't get as wet on the floor. There's lots of spray. He gonna be okay?' he asks, tilting his head toward Lawrence while he looks at Gerald. Gerald is wrapping a plastic bread bag around his camera.

'Yes, yes, he'll be fine,' Sophie says. She is beaming and nodding at her son. 'The bumpier and wetter the better.'

There is some shuffling and a small cry of surprise from Sophie when the seat of her shorts hits a pocket of water on the bottom of the raft, but they're all settled on the floor in thirty seconds.

Within minutes, they hit the rapids.

At the first bump, Kristen, grinning, looks sideways at Brent. Brent's eyes are round, and his mouth is like a rip in his face, an expression of surprise, or shock, a grey slash in the middle of his face. Kristen slides closer to him.

'What's wrong?'

Brent finally turns to her. He says something, but Kristen can't hear him because of the roar of the water.

'What?' she yells, turning her head so her ear is near his mouth. But she still can't hear anything. She looks at Rick, but his face is a knot of concentration, his eyes fixed on the buckling white mass of foam in front of them as he crouches, one knee on the edge of the raft, both hands gripping the paddle in its oarlock.

She turns back to Brent, glancing at the other three passengers. They are sitting calmly, small smiles turning up the sides of their mouths. They are looking at the landscape as it slides by. They seem unaware of any threat of danger.

Kristen is suddenly reminded of the three monkeys, the hear no, see no, speak no evil troika. But Gerald and Sophie and Lawrence do not raise their hands to cover their ears from the deafening roar, do not cover their eyes from the sickening swirling and foaming of the white water. They do not cover their mouths to keep from shrieking in terror. They sit, and smile, and observe, enjoying their ride on the Snake. They have complete trust, or are completely unafraid. Kristen decides it is the latter. She can imagine that Sophie and Gerald have faced demons before.

And Lawrence, well, Lawrence – he still sits in the middle, his arms pressed against his parents. Their warm flesh tells him, as always, that he is not alone, that he is safe.

Kristen reaches along the rope for Brent's hand. When she finds it, it's wet and cold, and clenched into a hard fist. She curls her own fingers over his, and squeezes. Brent looks at her.

She smiles, raising one eyebrow. 'This is fun, isn't it?' she yells, still smiling.

Under her palm, she feels Brent's hand grip the rope even tighter. She twists her neck and looks over at their hands, joined on the rope, and then looks back at Brent. Now his eyes are closed, and his lips are moving, but barely.

He's praying, Kristen thinks, the thought coming out of nowhere and thudding against her temple. He's praying.

She can't believe she didn't realize this before, didn't read into his hesitancy about coming on the rafting trip, his crankiness last night and this morning. Didn't ask, or make him tell her why he didn't want this holiday to be any of her ideas, all including lakes, instead of the dusty cowboy city of Jackson Hole. She tries to think of other times they've been around water. The only things she can think of are some Saturdays or Sundays at a nearby beach, where they lay in the sun or walked up and down the wet sand, prodding at shells and pieces of driftwood with their toes. Of the few Sundays at her friends Cindy and James', out in the suburbs. While she dove and swam lengths and then floated around the chlorinated aqua water on an air mattress, Brent and James sat on lawn chairs in the shade, drinking beer and occasionally checking the barbecue.

She looks at him again. His eyes startle open as if he had read her mind, as if he knew she had guessed his secret.

He's afraid of water, Kristen thinks again. An unexpected power surges through her, filling her chest. Then the power is replaced by a warm, deeper feeling. Finally. She has found a weakness, and for one instant she's glad. So glad that she knows this; it's easier to like him again. She takes her hands away from the rope, and turns her body to Brent, putting her hands on his thighs. She needs to tell him this, right now, needs to say that she likes him. Not to be afraid. He'll be fine. She's right here, beside him.

The raft gives one more up and down motion, this one bigger than the last, so high and then coming down so fast that for a second Kristen feels her stomach, and the contents of it, slide thick and greasy up her throat. She grabs for the rope she has let go of to lean towards Brent, but she is being tossed too violently, and can't catch on to the slippery yellow, and then, there is something else, a lurching movement that is very different from the rhythmic lift and drop. She hears Rick shout, and the shout echoes in her ears as the raft keeps going, lifting higher and higher out of the water, and finally down again, and then it's gone from beneath her, just gone. Kristen is propelled into the air, keeps going, as if an unseen giant hand had plucked her, easily as a doll, and then she is dropped, slapped rudely, deep into the water. She is too shocked to be afraid; it happens too quickly.

But then there is a longer time of growing panic when Kristen is under the water, swirling and tumbling, and then another few seconds of sheer terror as she is paddling, kicking her feet with all her might, and she fears she may be pushing herself down, instead of up, toward the surface. She tries to open her eyes, but the water is too hard, too cold, pushing against her closed eyelids with sharp jagged fingers. She finally bursts free of the heavy lid of water, bursts into air with the crash and shatter of breaking glass over her head. She takes a deep gulp, coughs, blinks to free her eyes of the cold sting, and is surprised to see that the water is quite calm again. She puts her hands to her neck to pull down the life jacket that is almost strangling her, rising high and tight around her jaw.

She turns her head in all directions, and sees the raft, and in it the dark round shapes of heads. She is mildly surprised she is so far away. She wonders if she was the only one thrown from the raft and then her thoughts tangle and fly to Brent. To Brent, who is afraid of the water, who was afraid of exactly this. She counts the heads. Four. Someone else is in the water.

Kristen starts to swim in the direction of the raft, even though the life jacket is restricting. She can feel the current, lazily pulling at her legs; it isn't too strong; she knows she is stronger. The raft, with its small convoy of heads, is moving, slowly but very steadily, downstream.

Suddenly she sees someone swimming toward her, swiftly, unencumbered by a life jacket. For one wild instant she thinks it's Brent, thinks she must have been mistaken about his fear, thinks he is coming to rescue her, or at least that he thinks he will be rescuing her, and she is annoyed. Annoyed that she was wrong.

But then she recognizes Rick. She waves at him. 'Go back, Rick. I'm okay. Go back,' she shouts, and she swims hard and strong, ignoring the bulkiness of the life jacket, to show him that she is telling the truth. And it is true. She knows she will make it to the raft with no problem. And now that she knows that the rest of them are safe, an overwhelming heady exhilaration fills her.

Rick stops for an instant, then turns his head back to the drifting raft. He looks at her again, and Kristen knows he is torn by this choice. 'Go back,' she yells, again, with as much authority in her voice as she can muster, 'go back to the raft. I'll make it there in a few minutes.' Rick floats for another second, then turns and swims away from her.

As she gets closer to the raft, Rick is clambering in over the side. He grabs the paddle and pulls hard, directing the raft towards her. Now she can see Brent, staring at her, but Kristen can't see any expression on his face. He is still gripping the rope; she can see his white hands on the yellow nylon.

By the way he suddenly turns his head, someone must have called his name. Kristen sees him looking at the other three passengers at the opposite end of the raft, at Gerald and Sophie, their boy still between them, safe. And then she sees Gerald's upper body move forward, one hand extending in Brent's direction. Kristen, slowly paddling her arms and swirling her legs, holds back from reaching the raft at this moment, watches as Brent closes his eyes and moves, inch by inch – it must be on his bottom – toward Gerald, and almost instantly he is close enough for Gerald to touch his cheek. Brent stops, and opens his eyes. He looks at Lawrence, with Sophie on the other side, and moves faster now, eyes open wide, until he is right beside Lawrence. Lawrence bobs his head at him, and their shoulders connect. Gerald settles down and closes the arc.

When Kristen finally swims to the edge of the raft, Rick holds out his hand and pulls Kristen the half metre, pulls her so her hand can reach up and hook onto the rope, then kneels on the edge, looking down at her.

'Hang on. I'll help you over. How're you doing? I saw you let go. I yelled at you to sit down, hang on. But you let go,' he says, now looking away from her, at the other passengers, letting them know it wasn't his fault, he wasn't responsible. He shakes his head to throw his wet hair out of his eyes. Kristen sees that his teeth are chattering.

She holds the rope with one hand while the other grips the slippery edge of the raft. She sees the faint stain of blue presenting itself under the white nails. The skin on the pads of her fingers is already softening. She studies her hands, watching them hang on, solid and sure. As the raft dips suddenly she looks up, and sees that Brent has left the safety of Gerald and Sophie and Lawrence and is coming toward her. His look is intent, so determined that his nose has thinned into a white beak. He crawls the short distance across the raft, his eyes never leaving hers, but testing before he sets down each palm, each knee, checking that the surface is solid enough to support his weight, as if he is crossing thin ice.

When he reaches her, he shakily sits upright, his bottom resting on his heels. He clutches the rope with one hand. The other he puts over hers on the edge of the raft.

Kristen looks at his earnest, distressed face, then down to his hand on hers. His knuckles, like his nose and the skin around his mouth, are chalky.

'You're sure you're okay?' he says, leaning toward her face.

She nods, then looks back to their hands. From nowhere, a lone dragonfly, its long turquoise tail trembling, touches down next to their joined hands.

The dragonfly rests there, on the hard wet rubber, and Kristen sees its slender body and strong jaws, sees her own face, a tiny, pale coin, in the insect's over-sized, almost cartoonish eyes.

And as she watches, the transparent wings, four of them, finely veined and fragile as newborn eyelids, vibrate for a moment, a shimmering blur. The dragonfly is not touching her; it is not the clinging darning needle of her childhood. They watch each other, Kristen and this delicate creature, and then, its visitation over, the dragonfly lifts gracefully. It rises, higher and higher, into the grey of the noon sky.

Kristen puts her head back to watch its ascent, water filling her ears and pulling gently at her hair, cradling her head in its cool embrace. She watches until it disappears, then looks back at Brent, who now grips her hand more firmly, ready to pull her up and in, beside him.

In a dark time, the eye begins to see.

– Theodore Roethke
In a Dark Time, 1964

The Summer Goldie Died

MY COUSIN MARSHA was a year and a half older than me, and Loreen and I were a few months apart. And we were bored that July, as only adolescent girls can be bored, our bodies hot and prickly and itching not only because of the heat, but because of something else – something that only Marsha seemed to know about for sure. She'd had a boyfriend, Garth, for the whole previous summer and into the fall – and, according to Loreen, they had spent a lot of time alone out on deserted country roads in Garth's father's pick-up. Since Garth, Marsha reported to me in a loud, jaded voice, she had had a number of boyfriends. Right now she was 'playing the field', going out with different boys until she decided which one she'd pick to go steady with. Had I ever had a boyfriend? she asked, unexpectedly, then immediately added, I didn't think so, one side of her mouth pulled up in a smirk, as I pretended great interest in the busy grooming of a bluebottle on the step beside me.

'Yeah,' Loreen said, looking at her sister, something like pride in her voice, 'Marsha had a different steady boyfriend every month since last summer, right, Marsha? And some of them are even finished school. Marsha only goes out with older boys. She won't go out with anyone unless they have a car, right, Marsha?'

I looked down the long lane that led from the main road, envisioning different coloured but identically rusted pick-up trucks coming and going, crunching over dead leaves in the fall, ploughing through the snowdrifts of winter and the oozing mud of spring, right on into this summer, driving up the long lane on the dry dust, honking their horns for Marsha as I had already seen them do a number of times since my arrival.

As well as having had many boyfriends, there was something else different about Marsha that summer – she had breasts. Large, soft, ballooning breasts that seemed to carry her forward, like a sail in the wind.

Loreen and I, both short and slight for fourteen, possessed, under our T-shirts, only the small hard nubs that reminded me of the beginnings of antlers on young deer.

I wasn't sure what it was I disliked so much about Marsha that summer, the boyfriends, the breasts, or something else I couldn't name. I looked at Marsha in a different light – and saw a different body and a new look on her face, a look of impatience and irritation. Marsha was impatient not only with Loreen and with me, but with the days themselves. They rarely varied; a round of collecting eggs and helping Auntie Tess with the big cooked breakfast of bacon or ham and the fresh eggs and sliced tomatoes and her home-made bread, then the dishes and by then there was laundry to hang on the clothes line and suddenly time to start lunch – again, way more food than I'd ever eaten for lunch in the city. It was only after lunch that we had a few hours to ourselves before the preparations for supper started.

But all of this seemed unimportant, at least to Marsha. It was the evenings that meant everything. Sometimes a boy even came to get her before we had our supper, Marsha racing to the car or truck, flinging a few words over her shoulder at Loreen to tell their mother she would eat in town or at so-and-so's house.

If no one had come by supper time, Marsha was hardly able to eat, waiting for the first plume of dust on the long lane, waiting for someone to come and pick her up. Unless you were going steady, planned dates didn't seem to be a country thing, according to Loreen – you either went into town and walked the main street, meeting up with friends, or waited at home, to see who would drop by. No one ever dropped by for Loreen, and the twice weekly we went into town didn't lead to anything for either of us, just endless walking up and down the uneven paving blocks in front of the stores that lined the street, eating ice-cream bars and paper cones of French fries until Auntie Tess and Uncle Mike had done their shopping and visiting and drove us home again, minus Marsha. She'd arrive much later, when the night was trying to cool down, the shrill of the crickets reverberating in waves that would stop at the sound of a vehicle pulling up, Marsha's loud laughter, the metal slam of a door and then the muted whoosh of tires going back down the dirt lane.

So during those endless afternoons, the waiting was clearly hard on her nerves, and she would grow more and more agitated, anticipating what the hot summer night might bring. She'd get snappish with Loreen and me, her eyes rolling at the sheer immaturity of our words and jokes as we sat on the top step of the landing at the unused front door of their two-storey frame house. The landing was just a splintery wooden rectangle, but the house cast shade on it in the afternoons, and, more importantly, it afforded a perfect view of the long, winding drive down from the main road that ran beyond the fields that bordered the farm.

Marsha would never join Loreen and me on the step. It was as if she had too much energy to sit still; she would walk around in front of us, stopping to extend a bare leg to admire the smooth-shaven gleam of her shin, holding her hands out in front of her to check the glossy sheen of her Avon Oyster Shell polish, pressing her upper arms against the sides of her body and then glancing down the front of her sleeveless cotton blouse to check the magnificent contour of her fairly new bosom. Marsha preened and strutted around that sunny, dusty yard every afternoon, confident and arrogant as one of Auntie Tess's prized Light Sussex hens. Those hens picked their way over the hard-packed dirt near the henhouse, lifting and then gingerly replacing their feet as if avoiding some unspeakable mess. They intrigued me with their aloof, haughty air, as if they were visitors, not really planning to stay, but merely putting up with the conditions they were forced into.

And, like me and like Marsha, the chickens ignored poor old Goldie, who lay near the barn in a small patch of shade in front of the piled fortress of hay bales that was her doghouse.

Goldie had lost whatever colour she had once been named

for. A cross between a Border collie and something else of indistinguishable parentage, she was a medium-sized dog with long, delicate white paws and sad, intelligent eyes grown rheumy. In the furious heat of that summer her lolling tongue was so huge and flaccid that it seemed an impossible task to keep it in her mouth. I remembered, from previous visits to the farm, Goldie's sneezy smile, how her black lips had stretched back from small pointed teeth, her tail swinging low, gracious, at my approach. I had vague memories of Goldie playfully chasing us around the yard, of dressing the patient dog in an old sweater and child's bonnet, of her dancing on slender hind legs for a tiny bite of some tidbit we had brought out from the kitchen.

But now she rarely rose from the shade, except to hobble to one side of her doghouse to squat in the dust, her head bowed with the embarrassment of having to relieve herself so close to her home, in so public a place. The patches of mange that had invaded her powdery coat revealed pink flesh so scaly and repulsive that I couldn't bring myself to touch her. Around her droned the constant buzz of flies.

During the first few days of my visit I chirped at her in a cheery, fake manner whenever I passed her, but her dulled eyes barely registered a flicker of interest. I must have known that she was dying, that she was too old to live much longer, but I didn't seem to care, or at least I don't remember caring, or thinking much about it.

Was I too caught up in my own nagging worry about what was going on in the city, back in my own clean box of a home?

I didn't want to spend my July here, at my aunt and uncle's farm. But I wasn't given a choice; I had been left there for four long weeks while my parents had 'time to themselves'. They needed this time to work things out, to try to keep their marriage together, and I was in the way. My parents were far too civilized to fight in front of me, and the festering issues would need to be aired in order to be cleansed and let new skin start to grow. My mother told me all of this in gentle terms, told me that she was sure she and Dad could work things out, if only they spent some time together, talking. Because of the seriousness of the huge implication, this possibility of divorce, I went, meekly and quietly, to Auntie Tess and Uncle Mike's farm. Frightened and slightly bewildered, I wanted to do everything in my power to keep my mother and father together, and this seemed the only chance I would be given.

And so I took a Greyhound to the town nearest my aunt and uncle's farm, and was picked up by my Auntie Tess, my mother's only sister, who acted as if my visit was a wonderful event that she and Uncle Mike and my cousins, Marsha and Loreen, were thrilled about. But Auntie Tess was the only one who could carry out this charade of joy at my arrival. When we stepped out of the car at the farm, Uncle Mike, in his usual reticent style, simply said hello and continued on his way out to the barn for evening milking. Marsha eyed me up and down, her gaze taking in my bushy hair, my matching madras shorts and blouse – the blouse clinging limply to my chest – and my obviously new and unsuitable white sandals. She made me feel, in that instant that her wide eyes travelled from my hair to my shoes, that I looked as awkward as I felt. Loreen only smiled shyly, not meeting my eyes and trying to stand behind Marsha.

The three of us, Marsha, Loreen and I, had all been born in the space of two years, and yet there had been little contact between us. Auntie Tess and Uncle Mike lived about sixty miles outside of the city. In my child's mind the sixty miles had seemed endless the few times I remembered driving out to the farm for a day visit during the summer holidays, and it made perfect sense that this alone would keep sisters and cousins apart.

I had always known that Auntie Tess and my mother were not at all alike, but I saw no reason for this to be a problem. My mother spoke little of her childhood or of her parents, dead long before I was even born; my father's family had more of an impact on me. They all came west frequently – my paternal grandparents and uncle and aunt – from their homes in Montreal to visit us. I was the only child in this family of adults, relegated to listening to grown-up conversations from around doorways and at the top of stairs. My grandparents and aunt and uncle were similar to my father and mother – reserved, soft-voiced, discussing books and films and politics. With me, my mother was always restrained and ladylike, her voice dropping to a modest whisper when she was forced to speak of such mundane issues as toilets or underwear. But with my grandparents and father's brother and sister she seemed to send off sparks, her eyes dancing, her laughter a little louder. Yes, with them my mother was at her brightest and best.

But those summer days we drove out to Tess and Mike's farm she grew silent and short-tempered. She walked through the yard and into the small house carefully, her shoulders high and stiff, as if at any moment she might see something shocking. Sitting in the sizable kitchen – it was the biggest room of the house, with a long marbled red Arborite table in the centre – my mother ate little of the meals I remember as huge and delicious. Those midday meals involved massive platters of meat, jugs of gravy, and steaming bowls of mashed potatoes and various kinds of beans – string, runner, and snap. My mother would take small, cautious bites, which she seemed to chew with her front teeth only, her lips firmly closed, and smile tightly at Marsha and Loreen as she chewed and swallowed and discreetly dabbed at her neck with her napkin. The kitchen was always hot. As well as an ordinary white electric stove, there was a woodstove in one corner; Auntie Tess said it was better for baking bread and pies, and of course there was fresh bread, and at least two pies baked in our honour.

She didn't seem bothered by the heat; Auntie Tess talked endlessly, laughing in shouts and snorts during the kitchen meals. There was one tall narrow window over the sink, always open on those summer visits. Plastic curtains, covered with dancing Dutch boys and girls in wooden shoes, fluttered at the unscreened opening. A long curly brown strip of flypaper, usually quite covered with the bodies of flies who had flown toward the smell of cooking meat, hung from the ceiling just in front of the window. As we passed the bowls and platters of food around the table, I would sometimes count how many of the flies were still weakly struggling on the sticky strip.

Auntie Tess's stories, as the meal slowed to the last few bites of pie crust, wouldn't stop. They became filled, in great detail, about situations that I realized later were probably appalling to my mother – the gory details of a neighbour's operation or the difficult birthing of a calf or the fitting of Uncle Mike's new dentures – and I was allowed not only to stay at the table throughout these tellings of tales, but also to ask questions and offer my own small contributions. Listening to me, Auntie Tess nodded and laughed, or leaned over and hugged me for no reason that I could see, and made me feel that I did, after all, have something interesting to say. And I loved her for that alone.

But that last summer of my parents' trouble, when the world around me was starting to take on a different hue, Auntie Tess no longer seemed the same. That summer I noticed, for the first time, the long tufts of black hair in her armpits; the way she wore the same yellow shorts day after day, and how they stretched too tightly across her wide, low bottom. Now her laughter took on the sound of a donkey bray, and I watched, with a repulsed fascination, as the fine strings of saliva caught between her square, strong front teeth when she opened her mouth, too wide, I also noted, as she ate. Yes, like I had with Marsha, I saw Auntie Tess in a different light that summer.

* * *

One of those interminable boring afternoons, when I thought longingly of the city, with its public swimming pools and air-conditioned theatres and cool bike trails near the river, Loreen said, suddenly, 'I know.'

Both Marsha and I looked at her with about as much interest as the chickens showed in Goldie. Loreen was not what was then referred to as retarded, but there was something not quite right about her. Once, driving home from one of the strained farm visits, when I was about ten, I realized my parents were discussing Loreen, and heard my father call her 'a bit slow', his voice hushed. I looked up to see my mother nod, then lowered my eyes again as she added, with a quick glance toward the back seat where I was reading my comic, 'But a lovely girl,' as if that made it all right to call Loreen slow.

At the same time that I was coming to the conclusion, that hot summer, that I didn't like Marsha, I was realizing how much I liked Loreen. I was in unspoken agreement with my parents that Loreen definitely seemed slow, although I couldn't, with any truth, call her lovely. But if I could have put a word to Loreen at that time, it would have been 'kindly'. At fourteen, I didn't think in terms like 'kindly', but looking back, I realize that word suited her.

And, as with everyone else except Uncle Mike, whom I never thought about in any way, I saw something different in Loreen that summer. While listening to her drowsy voice, watching her sluggish movements, I realized that she contained absolutely no malice, harboured no mean thoughts. That she never spoke rudely about anyone.

What I saw in particular was how she looked after Goldie, making sure her water dish was never empty, taking out the tin pie plate of meal leftovers after supper each night, pulling any meat off the bones first, to make it easier for Goldie. One evening, when the shadows had just started to stretch and a tease of cool air blew down from the hills north of the farm, I even saw Loreen sitting outside Goldie's doghouse with an old curry comb, brushing, with gentle, torpid strokes, the matted hair that the dog still possessed.

But in the same way that Loreen displayed no uncharitable thoughts or actions, she also rarely said anything of any great interest. So I waited, with little hope, to hear what she had to say, what it was she thought she knew. She turned her eyes toward me in a delayed, deliberate manner, as she always did. It seemed to me that her eyes waited to recheck, to verify the inner commands before they actually made their move. And

Loreen's eyelashes usually had a slightly gummy look, although I had often seen her methodically scrubbing her face with a washcloth in the bathroom. She actually spent a lot of time cleaning and grooming herself, but nevertheless, for all her washing and brushing of teeth and hair and changing of clothes, she gave off a slightly oily smell, something that seemed to come from within, and wouldn't be controlled by any amount of soap or talcum.

'We could go out to the old Mueller place,' she said now, the outer corners of her eyelashes sticking together and then pulling apart as her eyes widened on the word 'Mueller'.

'Who wants to go there?' Marsha said, ceasing her restless circling for a moment, smoothing her shorts down on her thighs. Her hands lingered longer than necessary on the soft flesh just above her knees.

Loreen shrugged and her eyes rotated in my direction. 'Barb hasn't been there yet. We could show her all the things.'

'What things?' I asked, lifting my hair off the back of my neck to let the air at it.

'The things they left. All their things.'

Marsha fingered the hem of one leg of her shorts. 'It's just a bunch of junk. Old furniture and stuff. There's nothing to see.' She turned toward the road as the far-off ticking of wheels echoed in the hushed afternoon. We all watched as a maroon Plymouth passed the lane in a billow of ochre dust.

Marsha's shoulder's slumped.

'Just the Barkers,' Loreen said, her voice apologetic. 'They only have a couple of little kids,' she added, an explanation for Marsha's disappointment. Then she stood, saying 'Come on, Marsha. If we hang around, we might have to go pick berries. Mom was talking about making pie. Let's go to the Muellers'.'

Marsha cast one more longing glance toward the empty stretch of road at the end of the lane. 'All right,' she agreed, her lips full and petulant. I saw that the lipstick she painstakingly applied, even to go out to get the eggs, had worn away. As if reading my thoughts, she reached into the pocket of her shorts and pulled out a green plastic tube, yanked off the top and wound the base. 'But I'm not going out to the old greenhouse. Remember that, Loreen. I'm telling you right now.' She rolled the cylinder of frosted pink back and forth over her bottom lip, then firmly pressed the top lip into it. 'I'm not going to the greenhouse,' she repeated, slipping the lipstick back into her pocket, 'so don't try and talk me into it.'

* * *

It took over an hour to get to the Mueller place, at least at the pace we walked, a long, broiling hour. We picked our way through a field of scratchy bearded barley, pushed through rows of waist-high corn, and finally plodded across an open pasture with a dried-out slough. We stopped and looked at the cracked mud at the bottom of the slough, and Loreen picked up a small rock and threw it into the middle. It landed with a soft thud, stirring up a small fury of more red dust. We all looked at the dust as if something might show itself, might rise, miraculously, from that dead earth, something to surprise us, thrill us, make us forget the heat and jar us from our apathy.

'We should have brought something to drink,' Marsha said. 'It's too hot.'

'We're almost there,' Loreen answered, and turned from the slough. Marsha and I followed her on a narrow, one-person path that led from the slough to a stand of stunted trees. As we passed through the quick dimness and then back out into the brilliant sunshine, I realized the trees were a windbreak.

'This is it,' Loreen said. We all stopped.

The farmhouse listed to the right, its wood siding an unpainted, silvery grey. All the windows were broken, and some had no glass left at all. There was a brown couch on the yellowed weedy patch in front of the house. Most of the couch's stuffing was pulled out but still attached, hanging in tufts and strings, reminding me of Goldie and her pitiful, mange-ravaged coat. There was a man's scuffed work boot, minus its tongue and lace, sitting on the sagging arm of the couch. Empty bottles, brown beer and clear vodka and gin, were scattered around it.

But more importantly, at least to Marsha, was that there was a car far off to the left, a two-tone station wagon with a cracked windshield.

'It's Buddy Abram's,' she said, all weariness gone from her voice. 'Buddy must be here, and probably Jeff.' She stood on her toes, her eyes searching the yard for them.

As if in answer, three bodies appeared in the doorway of a frame of broken glass that stood about a hundred yards from the house. From that distance, all I could tell was that the bodies were male, and were tall and skinny, all with short hair in varying degrees of brown.

'Hi! Hi, guys!' Marsha called, waving, her voice light. She quickly patted at her hair, smoothed down her shorts. 'Do I look okay?' she whispered, turning to Loreen and me, as if the boys could hear from so far away. She pulled out her lipstick.

We both nodded.

Then she looked at the greenhouse, at the figures in the doorway, and back to us. 'Why don't you show Barb the house, Loreen? Go on, Barb, you'll like it,' she said, rolling a thick layer of pink on her lips. 'They were Nazis, the Muellers.'

'They were not,' Loreen said in a weary, non-argumentative voice. 'You know they weren't Nazis, Marsha. They were just German. That's what Dad says. They were just a German family.'

'They were Nazis,' Marsha said, with a tone of finality that neither Loreen nor I could hope to contest. She started away from us, across the littered yard. 'I'm going to go see what's going on over there.'

'But they're in the greenhouse, Marsha,' Loreen said, her voice rising. 'You don't like the greenhouse.'

Marsha raised one shoulder in a shrug and kept going. 'See you in a while,' she said, without turning her head, so that we could hardly hear her.

We watched her go, her footsteps, while still slow, no longer heavy and tired; there was a new rhythm now.

'Come on, Barb, come on,' Loreen said, pulling at my arm. 'Come inside and look.'

The air was still, silent. Birdless. Not even the croak of a frog, the creak of a katydid. In spite of the sweat between my shoulder blades, I could feel a shiver start somewhere behind me, on the tops of my arms, the back of my head.

'What is this place, anyway?'

'It's the Mueller place,' Loreen said.

'I know *that*,' I said. 'But what *is* it?'

'Come inside, and you'll see.'

I followed Loreen toward the house, wiping the sweat off my upper lip. We wedged ourselves through the doorway, the warped wooden door permanently stuck in its half welcoming, half forbidding position, and I was momentarily blind in the semi-darkness of the house's interior. As my eyes adjusted, I saw that the inside of the house was as ruined as outside. Pieces of broken furniture and torn books covered the floor, mixed with shattered glass from dishes and windows. There were more empty liquor and beer bottles. The whole place had an eerie, unreal atmosphere, and I experienced a rush of guilt, like we were trespassing, spying on something that didn't want to be seen.

I stooped and picked up one of the books. The writing wasn't in English, but it seemed that it might be a Bible. The pages were so soft and light they were almost transparent. On the front page there was a lot of strange writing, with numbers following each line. Dates, maybe. I put the book on a dusty shelf attached to one wall.

'Let's go upstairs,' Loreen said. 'There are still baby clothes and pictures up there.'

I didn't want to see baby clothes and pictures. It was awful, this destroyed house with all the remains of a family. But I followed Loreen up the narrow set of stairs, right into a bedroom with a low, slanting roof. In it was a metal crib, and, as Loreen had said, a number of tiny clothes, strewn everywhere. There was a small, strange wooden object with metal wheels that probably had been some kind of toy. I walked into the adjoining room, identical to the first. In this room was another rusted metal bed frame, a double. A filthy mattress lay on the floor beside the bed frame. There were a few photos, black-and-white, under fly-specked and cracked glass, lying on the top of a wooden dresser. One was a wedding picture; another showed a woman holding a small child on her lap. On the wall over the bed frame, a swastika was etched on the faded flowered wallpaper, drawn with what looked to be something dark and charred.

Looking at the swastika and the ripped-up mattress and the photographs, I suddenly found it hard to breathe in the small, stifling room, and went to the open window and leaned out. I could see the sun reflecting off the few unbroken panes in the roof of the greenhouse.

'Why is Marsha afraid of the greenhouse?' I asked, turning around to Loreen. She had brought the wooden toy in from the other bedroom and was running her fingers over one of the wheels, spinning it.

'My dad says nobody around here ever saw a greenhouse before,' she said. 'But the Muellers had one, at home in Germany, and Mr Mueller built one here for his wife. So she wouldn't be so homesick.' Loreen set the toy on the floor and pushed it with her toe. It rolled forward a few inches.

'When I was younger, I used to be afraid to go there, too,' she continued. 'But then me and Marsha finally went in, and I found some flowers still growing there. Not in pots, but in the ground. That was before the place got broken up so bad. There were all kinds of flowers growing in the shade under the tables. I brought some home once, and Mom said they must have fallen from the tables and gone wild.'

'But why were you afraid of it? Why is Marsha still afraid?'

'It's supposed to be haunted.'

I looked back out the window. The glare on the glass roof hurt my eyes.

'Mrs Mueller killed herself there, after their baby died,' Loreen said, pushing at the toy again. 'She hung herself. And then Mr Mueller went away. He left everything, Dad said, even the food on the table. There wasn't a funeral, and Dad said he heard Mr Mueller took Mrs Mueller's body with him. Back to Germany. But Mom said that part's probably not true.'

'Creepy,' I said, wanting to leave this place more than before. 'Let's go and get –' I started to say, but jumped as an engine roared to life outside.

Loreen and I both looked out, seeing the station wagon careening down the road beside the greenhouse.

'I hope Marsha didn't go with them,' Loreen said. 'It's her turn to do dishes tonight. If she went we'll be stuck with them.'

We clattered down the stairs and outside. I felt a strange sense of relief to leave that sad and shattered place. As we got close to the greenhouse, Loreen called out.

'Are you still here, Marsha? Marsha?' Her face fell. 'She must have gone with them,' she said, stopping at the doorway.

I stayed back. I could imagine a body hanging there, the neck broken and head tilted to one side, maybe the tongue out, motionless in the still, dead afternoon air in the greenhouse. Were flowers blooming on the tables when she did it? Did the tips of her shoes brush against soft petals as she twitched and jerked in her final moments? To Loreen and Marsha the death of Mrs Mueller was old news. To me it was fresh and horrible.

As I made gruesome pictures in my head, Loreen said one word. 'Marsha,' she exhaled, in a breathy whisper.

I took a step forward, and could see Loreen's usually florid face draining of colour. Her eyes were wide, and unblinking. The small cold shivers I'd had from the minute I walked into the Mueller house grew stronger, seemed to gather, gaining force and momentum. The cold rushed to my hands and feet, and I felt my back teeth grinding together painfully. I was afraid to look. But I did, over Loreen's shoulder.

Marsha hadn't driven off with the boys. She was there, on the floor, propped against an overturned wooden table. All of the tables that had once held pots were smashed and broken except for one. It stood boldly in the middle of the greenhouse, and for one absurd moment I thought that must be the one Mrs Mueller had climbed on and then jumped off, the thick braided twine tightening around her slender neck. Then I looked away from the table, back to Marsha. There were chunks and shards of glass from the roof on the floor, everywhere, mixed in with scrubby weeds and foxtails and rough grass. There were no more flowers growing wild in that soil, even though, in the dry hot smell of the greenhouse, I thought I caught a whiff of their decay. There was only glass, and weeds, and beer bottles. Some weren't empty, lying on their sides as dark wet patches grew in the soft dirt around them. The sun was magnified by all the glass, surrounding Marsha with a shimmering aura of brightness.

The skin of her face, and her neck and chest, so clear in that bright light, was red and splotchy. Her blouse, the pink one with the white daisies, had a big rent at the collar, and it was open, the buttons ripped completely off. One strap of her white bra was ripped loose from its plastic clasp, and the cup hung down, empty, leaving her left breast exposed. I tried to draw my eyes away from that large, luminous globe, but it seemed difficult. I don't know why I wanted to look at her breast, I just did. I can still see it, today, in my mind, its shape and the heavy, weighed-down, somehow defeated look of it. Her lipstick was smeared all around her mouth, and onto one cheek, and her right hand was cut across the fleshy pad right below the thumb, and she was holding it up, her other hand supporting her elbow. She was looking at the blood running down her wrist, staring at it, tears bunched and clinging, trembling on the ends of her mascaraed lashes, but not dropping, not running down her face. She seemed more fascinated with the flow of her blood than anything.

'Marsha!' Loreen said, going to her. 'Marsha! What happened?' Her voice had a light, high sound, verging on what I thought, at the time, was laughter, but realized later was something like hysteria. She, too, stared at the blood, then looked around, on the ground, as if searching for something. She finally looked at me, and her eyes travelled to my hair.

'Give me your scarf,' she said, staring at the pale green cotton square I had folded and twisted and put around my head and tied under my hair at the back.

I pulled it off and walked over to Loreen. Small pieces of glass crunched beneath my feet, with a tinkly, almost cheerful sound. I handed my scarf to her, and she untied the knot and wrapped the scarf around and around Marsha's hand. Then she pulled the strap of Marsha's bra up and fiddled with it for a moment, finally fixing it in place. I felt an immediate sense of relief, and the feeling that things were somehow in control again, once I could no longer look at Marsha's breast.

Next Loreen examined Marsha's blouse, holding the torn edges near the collar together for a moment, then pulling the front closed, although as soon as she took away her hands it fell open again. Marsha let Loreen carry on around her with a kind of calm resignation.

'Let's go home, Marsha,' Loreen said. 'Come on.' She gently wiped Marsha's face with the heel of her fist, but faint streaks of lipstick still showed. Then Loreen took Marsha's hand, the unhurt one, and Marsha obediently got to her feet.

'Wait until I tell,' Loreen said. 'Wait until I tell what those boys did.' Her eyes blinked once, slowly. Apart from giving Loreen my headscarf, it was as if I didn't exist. Neither of them said anything to me, or looked at me.

'No, don't,' Marsha whispered. 'You can't, don't,' she repeated, a little louder, as if her voice was returning from some faraway place. 'Don't,' she said, for the third time, and by this time her voice had fully returned. It had that same unquestionable authority she had used when declaring that the Muellers were Nazis. 'Dad will kill me. You know he will, Loreen. So just don't say anything.'

'But Marsha, those boys were mean to you. Buddy and Jeff and Ricky. They ripped your blouse, and ...' Loreen's voice trailed off. The vision of Marsha's breast seemed to fill the air in front of me.

'Your hand, you'll have to show Mom your hand, Marsha,' Loreen added. 'There might be glass in it.' We all looked at

Marsha's hand, seeing the bloom of red soaking through the pastel material. The silence grew. 'But you can wait by the barn, and I'll bring you another blouse first,' Loreen said, and I realized that she had just agreed to do what Marsha had instructed, not to tell, to keep this secret, although it was clear Loreen didn't understand what the secret was.

I knew; I could imagine what had happened, Marsha teasing and laughing and thrusting her body at those boys the way I had seen her so many times in town on the hot, dust-filled evenings. I could imagine the boys, their laughter turning to something else that none of them would have thought of if they'd been alone, could imagine Marsha's horror when they would not stop. The heat and images of Marsha and the three boys grew huge in my head; they were ugly, but at the same time sent a strange, somehow pleasurable weakness through my groin and thighs. And I hated Marsha even more, at that moment, for what she had made me think about, blamed her for making me feel excited by the blood and the idea of violence and by having to stare at her large woman's breast and feeling that in some way my thoughts would be discovered and I would be punished. The images throbbed and ached in my temples.

'Let's go home, Marsha,' Loreen said again, a quaver in her voice.

We walked back, Marsha occasionally stumbling as she stepped into shallow gullies and tripped over stones in the fields. She didn't seem aware of the ground under her feet. But I was. Every step sent a pounding all the way up from my feet through my body to add to that beating in my head. Everything looked and felt too clear, too bright, everything exaggerated, from the grasshoppers throwing themselves against my bare arms and legs and the cut of each sharp blade of long coarse grass on my ankles to the hot wind in my nostrils and down my throat.

We detoured around the yard to come up beside the barn.

'Wait here,' Loreen said, and left. Marsha looked over at Goldie's house, and I looked, too. Then she didn't wait, as

Loreen had told her, but walked over to Goldie. I still felt invisible, as if I were some outside viewer, not part of the whole scene that kept unfolding in front of me. It was as if I could come or go, speak or not speak, and it wouldn't make any difference. No one would notice or care. So I followed Marsha.

The old dog seemed asleep, tongue still protruding. But the tongue was stiff now, purple, a fly busily crawling over it. Marsha, holding her blouse closed with her bandaged hand, suddenly sat down beside the dog, her back against the harsh prickle of the hay. And I saw that Goldie was not asleep, but dead. I could just tell.

I looked at Marsha, but her head was down, her legs straight out in front of her. Her hand still held her blouse closed. The Light Sussex hens high-stepped around the two of them.

Then, without any warning, Marsha let her blouse go and started to cry, soundlessly, cradling Goldie's head in her lap, heedless of the mange, of the dark, swollen tongue. I stood looking down on them, my own arms rigid at my sides, seeing the working of Marsha's throat and the heaving of her chest, the mottled imprints on her upper arms and the tops of her breasts turning from red to a deeper burgundy that I knew would be bruises tomorrow.

I heard Loreen come up behind me, recognizing the slight shuffle of her steps. But I didn't turn, and she stayed there, behind me. I could hear her breathing, and I could smell her, not the usual oily smell, but something else, something stronger, and thicker. And as I listened and inhaled, I knew someone else was there, too, breathing in unison with Loreen.

I knew it must be Auntie Tess, and then also knew that maybe for the first time in her life, Loreen had not done what Marsha told her. She had used her own judgement, and told their mother. And before the realization could fully sink in, before I could mentally give Loreen a sudden new respect, Auntie Tess moved in front of me, toward Marsha. Her steps were quick now, with an unfamiliar spring. Her mouth was closed, and I realized I had hardly ever seen it closed; whenever I saw Auntie Tess she was talking or laughing or eating. But with it closed, it looked smaller, softer, and I was reminded of my mother, and suddenly I missed her, my mother, and the ache I felt in wanting her at that moment shocked me. I started to cry, standing in that hot, hot, sun, watching while Auntie Tess crouched beside Marsha and the still body of ancient Goldie.

* * *

My mother phoned, last week, to tell me that Auntie Tess had died of cervical cancer. It had come on very quickly, apparently, only three weeks from diagnosis to death. She went that fast, my mother said, and Mike was in real shock up at the farm, thank goodness he had Loreen there with him. My mother was going to fly back for the funeral; I had just returned to my lecturing job at the university after my last maternity leave, and couldn't take any time off. I didn't really even consider going; I hadn't had any contact with any of them, Tess or Mike, Marsha or Loreen, since that summer, only hearing from my mother that Auntie Tess always asked after me and said to say hello in her yearly Christmas card.

My mother gave me the phone number at the farm, and I dialled. The carefully measured 'Hello?' was instantly recognizable as Loreen's, even after all these years. While I expressed my sorrow at her mother's death, Loreen interrupted a few times to thank me for calling, seeming shy, nervous, almost apologetic that I had phoned from such a distance, mentioning more than once that this call would cost me an arm and a leg, especially as it was in the middle of the day. There was little to say after I offered my condolences and we each talked about our children, their ages and activities.

I asked about Marsha, finally, and Loreen said she was arriving the next day, just before the funeral. It had been difficult tracking her down, as Marsha had moved around a lot, and Loreen considered it lucky to have found her at all, and in time for the funeral.

Marsha hadn't been in touch with them for more than a decade, according to Loreen, as the older girl and her mother had had some sort of falling out, years ago, and Marsha hadn't phoned or written any of them since then. I didn't ask why, but I found it hard to imagine; I couldn't think of what could possibly have happened between Auntie Tess and Marsha to warrant this alienation.

And as I hung up the phone, all I could remember was how Goldie had looked, dead in Marsha's lap, and the surprising uncertain line of Auntie Tess's mouth as she lifted the dog's body away and studied her daughter's face.

What we take to be our strongest tower
of delight, only stands at the caprice of the
minutest event – the falling of a leaf, the
hearing of a voice, or the receipt of one
little bit of paper scratched over with a
few small characters by a sharpened feather.

– Herman Melville
Pierre, 1852

Quoth the Raven

SHE IS CRYING. At first Bill isn't sure if those are tears on her cheeks, because the fine London drizzle that has been falling for the last week gives everything a soft, damp look. Almost airbrushed, as if this gentle, moist air is briefly erasing the usual city soot and grime. And so the girl's cheeks look a little wetter than everyone else's, and it is really her eyes that Bill has to study to see if he's right. Watching her, he brushes his fingertips over the feather, a long, shiny black feather he has found on the cobblestones at his feet. Bill notices that the girl doesn't even glance at the Yeoman Warder who is giving the small group this late-September tour of the Tower of London. Instead, she keeps looking around her, the tears running down her cheeks, but her mouth and chin firm.

She lowers her head, changing the set of her shoulders. And in that instant something about the tender map of her scalp, just visible in the scrambled nest of shorn hair, makes Bill sick with hope, with longing. It keeps happening. Of course, he tells himself, it's only natural. Everywhere he looks he sees girls, young women really, that might be her. This girl is younger than his daughter; she looks about sixteen or seventeen. But the number of times he had seen his own girl standing in front of him, head dropped, shoulders slumped, cheeks wet with tears, like this unknown girl, were too many to count.

The girl is alone. She stands off to one side of the group, her bulging backpack stained and streaked with dirt and who knows what else. He tries to concentrate on the uniformed man's words, but they seem a jumble of facts and confusing trivia.

There is a small swell of laughter from the crowd. Bill misses the joke but smiles, glancing at the girl. She has raised her head, but instead of looking at the Yeoman Warder, is staring up at the imposing tower to the left, the one that Bill knows, from his brochure, to be the White Tower. There are so many towers. Riding the underground to the Tower Hill station, Bill had counted the ones named in the Tower of London brochure he had picked up from the rack in his hotel lobby. The Tower of London, it is called, the Tower. But there are over twenty of them, from the Inner Ward towers, some prisons or dungeons or places of murder, like Wakefield Tower and Salt Tower and the infamous Bloody Tower where the little princes had met their death, to the Outer Ward towers, whose functions were more domestic and less brutal. Bill had read as much information as possible during the long, swaying ride, trying to force his thoughts to somewhere other than the address on the paper in his breast pocket.

As the group moves on, he stays still for a few seconds so that he will be at the back, nearer the girl. Eventually she walks past him, and surprising himself, Bill holds the feather out, saying, 'Leave no black plume as a token of that lie thy soul hath spoken.'

Her head spins in his direction, and in that instant it's as if she's taken her hand and swiped it over her face, changing it in the way of mimes or some television impersonator. Her eyes, light gold, almost topaz when filled with tears, clear, harden into a brassy brown, and her lips compress to form a harsh crease. Bill feels himself recoiling, as if she has hissed an obscenity under her breath. Her face is closed, ageless, now. She stares into his eyes, then lets her eyelids drop a fraction, and Bill relaxes under that familiar adolescent glare he remembers so well. Then she turns her head away, her shoulder rising in an exaggerated, irritated twitch, and she marches off.

Oh God, Bill thinks. He wants to take it back, or explain to her what he'd meant, say something to reassure this girl that it's only a line of poetry, that it's just a line, but it isn't a *line*, nothing like that. That it's because she reminds him of his daughter, that's all. But it's quite clear that she has the wrong idea. How he must look to her! A middle-aged man, alone, following a pack of tourists with the hope of picking up a woman young enough to be his daughter.

But even as he's thinking all of this, he knows he can't explain himself, can't explain how he wants to be near her, absorb some of her, let her youth and her vulnerability and her tough act remind of him why he can't give up. Not now, not after all this time, not when he's so close.

He moves around to the other side of the group, away from the girl. He shouldn't be here, not at the Tower of London, doing this completely absurd sightseeing thing, as if he were here on a holiday, as if he were an ordinary tourist. But when he woke up this morning, and thought about the last lead, the youth hostel in the East End, he was too afraid.

This afternoon, he had told himself over his breakfast on a tray in his room, I'll go this afternoon, when I'm up to it. So he had decided to visit the Tower of London, to do one unplanned thing, something that might take his mind off what he was doing in London, what hope he had pinned on this journey.

He tries to stay away from the girl, not even glancing in her direction, until the Yeoman Warder starts to talk about the ravens.

'By tradition,' the man says, pointing to a flapping cluster of huge, slick black birds in an area of well-tended grass, 'there have always been ravens at the Tower of London. Initially the scavengers most likely flew in to feed off the abundant refuse of the first Tower inhabitants. The ravens link England's past with her future. Six of the large black birds are always within the Tower's walls. They are tended to by the Yeoman Raven-master. Their presence has been protected by the legend predicting that when the last raven has left the Tower of London, the Tower will fall – and the kingdom with it.'

Bill reads the sign at the edge of the grass – NO PICNICKING – and under it, another – RAVENS BITE. He studies the birds, who ignore the visitors and haughtily pick their way through the crisp grass, seeking and pecking and digging. The Yeoman Warder's clipped British voice rises and falls sharply. 'I stated that the traditional number of ravens is six, but as you can see, there are nine. With all the calamities befalling the Royal Family in these times, they want additional assurance.' The group laughs, and Bill catches a motion out of the corner of his right eye as the girl moves into his line of vision.

'Their wings are clipped, naturally,' the Yeoman Warder reports.

'Naturally.' Bill hears the echo, just to his right, but he doesn't look at her. The group begins their walk to Traitors' Gate. Bill and the girl are the last stragglers. When the Yeoman Warder begins to explain the significance of the gate, Bill turns his head casually, afraid that anything sudden might make her withdraw.

Now he realizes that she is older than he had thought. Maybe she is as old as his daughter, after all. But there is a look about her, that hardness in her eyes and mouth that his daughter doesn't have. Didn't have, Bill corrects himself. Not the last time he saw her.

The girl meets and holds his gaze, and Bill sees he has been granted another chance. He looks down at her hands, her reddened fingers, the nails bitten to the skin. He offers the feather. The girl studies it, not reaching for it, and Bill says, in a voice that draws a circle around the two of them, 'For the rare and radiant maiden whom the angels name Lenore – Nameless here for evermore.'

The girl starts, and her hand flies up to her mouth. Before Bill has a chance to ask what's wrong, she rasps through her fingers, 'How did you know?' Her cheeks are spread with colour; it rises up so that even her eyebrows seem to darken.

'I'm sorry,' Bill answers. 'It's only a quote, from a poem. I don't know anything.' He pushes the feather toward her, hoping she will take it, that her acceptance of it will repair whatever damage he has unwittingly done again. The Yeoman Warder and the group walk away from the gate. Bill and the girl don't move.

'My name,' the girl says. 'How do you know my name?'

'I don't know your name.' Bill shakes his head.

'Lenore. Lenore,' she repeats, louder. 'Except everyone calls me Lonnie.'

'It's from Edgar Allen Poe's poem, "The Raven", Bill says. 'Actually, when I picked up the feather, I didn't know about the ravens here. The words from the poem – black plume – just popped into my mind, and out of my mouth.'

'I thought you were some pervert. Lots of them around.'

'No ... you look ... no,' Bill says. 'My name is William. William Nelson Lawton. Except everyone calls me Bill.'

'You American?'

'Canadian,' he answers. He tries a smile, puts the feather into his left hand and holds out his right.

'Canada? Never been there.' Lonnie looks at his hand, shrugs, then shakes it.

Bill feels the coldness of her thin fingers. 'Everyone's over at the Chapel now,' he says, when they drop their hands. 'Do you want to go and see it?'

'No. I don't listen to all that stuff, anyway. I'm leaving London today, and I wanted to come here first. Just to see it, get the feel of the place. I don't care about details. All I'm looking for is the feel, what I pick up.' She wipes at her nose with the back of her hand. 'So. I should go.' She jerks her upper body, an easy practised motion that resettles her backpack straps on her shoulders. 'Nameless,' she says. 'Freaky. About Lenore ... and all that.' She turns.

'Lonnie,' Bill says, and she looks back. 'Have you been okay, travelling around by yourself? Do you feel all right at the hostels, the shelters? Is that where you stay? Are they really safe? Safe places?'

Lonnie's lids start to lower again. 'What do you mean?'

Bill looks down at the feather. The silence has a sound of its own.

'Poor things,' Lonnie finally says. 'Having their wings clipped so they can't fly, can't do what they need to do. So they're stuck here, forever.' She pauses, then, 'Evermore. Stupid, to do something like that for the sake of tradition.'

Bill looks straight ahead, at one of the narrow windows in

the wall in front of him. 'Tradition means a lot to some people.'

Lonnie lifts her chin in the direction of the grass and the ravens. 'Did anyone stop to think what those birds would rather be doing, give them a choice about spending their whole lives here – here,' she waves her hand at the mossy stone walls, 'in this ivory tower?'

'White Tower,' Bill says.

'Whatever.'

'But these are the lucky ones, Lonnie. They have everything. Everything is given to them. Food, shelter. They're protected from harm.'

'Yeah. By the Ravenmaster. The name says it all.'

'I thought you didn't listen,' Bill says. 'And besides, they're just birds. Maybe they don't want any more than this.'

'Right. Just birds,' Lonnie says. Her eyes move down to his polished loafers, beading with droplets, back up to his thick greying hair. 'What are you doing here, anyway?'

Bill puts out one hand and runs his fingertips over the time-worn smoothness of the stones. 'Looking for someone.'

Lonnie gives a small snort. 'Aren't we all.' It is not a question. 'Well, good luck. Me, I'm on to warmer places. Heading south. Greece for the winter.'

'Greece,' Bill says. 'You be careful, now.'

Lonnie nods once, then walks away from Bill, her head swivelling as she looks up at the high walls on either side of her.

'Lonnie. Lenore!' Bill calls, once more.

She stops.

'Do you want the feather?'

Lonnie shakes her head. 'You keep it, William Nelson Lawton. Keep it. Or give it to someone who needs it.'

Bill studies the feather, and just before the girl turns the corner, says, 'I will.' He's not sure if she heard him. Then he puts the feather in the left breast pocket of his jacket so it won't get wet in the rain that is now coming down in a steady, pulsing rhythm, turning the grey stone to glistening silver.

Deceive not thyself by overexpecting happiness in the married state.... Remember the nightingales which sing only some months in the spring, but commonly are silent when they have hatched their eggs.

– Thomas Fuller
The Holy State and the Profane State, 1642

When Birdie Came

IT WAS THE FALL of 1968 when Birdie came to the house on Dunvegan Road in Forest Hill.

The first two women sent by the O'Hara Employment Agency to the beautiful house with the velvet lawn and perfectly sculpted flower beds didn't work out.

Margaret had been loud and clumsy, breaking one of Nadine's Limoges demitasses – part of the set from an antique store on King – the very first day, and keeping the radio in the kitchen turned up high to the phone-in talk shows, all morning. She also whistled as she stomped around the house, a harsh, tuneless, masculine whistle, and it got on Nadine's nerves. Margaret had lasted three weeks.

The second woman, Annette, was very religious, and had stayed longer, almost two months. Nadine would have kept her on; Annette was a hard worker, and quiet and careful, but the children complained.

Annette thought that the children shouldn't be watching so much television and listening to the kind of music they did. She hid Kevin's records in stacks of magazines and once threw out a new book of Andrea's, a book called *The Carpetbaggers*, flipping through it and deciding it wasn't appropriate reading for Andrea. She moved things around in their room, outraging them at what they called an invasion of their space. And they both said her breath smelled of something dead and rotting, and swore she didn't flush the toilet after she'd used it. While Nadine recoiled from Annette's breath, and wondered if the woman had stomach trouble, she hadn't noticed anything unusual about her bathroom habits.

Nadine found it difficult to call the agency the second time and say that things hadn't worked out. She didn't want them to think that she was a complainer. She carefully explained that it was her children that had a problem with Annette, that possibly Annette wasn't used to the ways of teenagers.

Nadine knew that the children just didn't like anyone coming into their house to help. They didn't want to help either, even though they were old enough – Margaret and Annette had mentioned to Nadine, more than once – to make their own beds and pick up their own dirty clothes off the floor. Nadine knew they were right, knew how hard she had been working when she was Andrea's age, keeping up with the eggs, and doing a grown woman's work in the house while going to school at the same time. And Kevin, well, Nadine wasn't sure what fourteen-year-old city boys should be doing; she did think, however, that he spent far too much time listening to music with his eyes closed. But she wasn't comfortable trying to discipline Kevin. Because she hadn't had any brothers, she didn't know much about men except for her father and then her husband. But she thought it wouldn't hurt Kevin to do a bit around the house either.

* * *

When Birdie comes, Nadine has the surprise of her life. She goes to the door when the doorbell chimes at exactly eight-thirty on the morning of September the fifteenth and, opening it, feels her smile, not exactly fading, but changing, minutely. She has to put her head back, and look up, higher than when she looks at Stephen, to study Birdie's smooth brown face, the heavy-lidded black eyes, the short round frizzle of her grey hair.

'Come in, come in,' Nadine says, forcing her smile back to its original size. 'You must be ... is it Birdie? The agency said Birdie.'

The woman nods. Her eyes stare at the top button of Nadine's blouse, and the younger woman feels herself blinking more than usual.

'Birdie, yes, well, Birdie. Come in.' Nadine steps back from the door, sweeping her arm out from her side as if she is a model on a game show, demonstrating the Laz-E-Boy recliner or queen-size orthopedic mattress that could be won.

Birdie steps into the foyer, looking around the spacious entry. She unbuttons her sweater and lifts her white leatherette purse off her arm.

'And where shall I be putting my things, Madam?' Birdie asks.

To Nadine, it sounds like she says 'my tings'.

'Oh, oh, yes,' Nadine says, 'I'll show you the room the other –' she stops herself, 'the room that we use for guests,' she finishes, although there have never been any guests. Then, as an afterthought, 'And please, you don't have to call me Madam. My name is Nadine.'

Birdie sets her purse on the floor and pulls her arms out of her cardigan. 'I prefer to call my ladies Madam or Missus,' she says.

'Oh. Well then, Missus, I suppose,' Nadine says, with a silly little laugh that slips out before she can stop herself. Birdie doesn't smile.

And while Nadine is showing Birdie the room upstairs where she can leave her purse and sweater, the small room with the narrow bed, the room beside the bathroom that the children use, she is thinking, what will Stephen say when I tell him about Birdie?

* * *

Nadine knows nothing of Stephen's true background. He fabricated a tidy story of his youth and dead parents to match his acquired name, and Nadine had no reason to suspect he wasn't telling the truth. Perhaps Nadine would have liked to know that her husband hadn't always been the immaculate, smooth-talking, soft-handed man she married. She might have liked to know Stanislaw, the little Stasui. Stephen might have endeared himself to her by confessing his love for the poppyseed roll his mother always made for him the day after an upset with his father. Or his fear of the harsh, shouted words of the priest in church every Sunday; his remembered humiliation of not knowing enough English, on his first day of grade one, to ask to go to the bathroom, and running all the way home at recess, over the streetcar tracks and past the baskets of fruit and vegetables outside the store fronts, then back again, crying the whole time.

But she didn't know these things about her husband, knew him only as a man who wasn't afraid of anything, had no insecurities about who he was and what he was doing with his life.

There was only one thing that occasionally puzzled her. She wasn't positive, but sometimes she thought she sensed something – almost like a stiffening – when they were out at a restaurant and were served by someone with an accent, an accent she didn't recognize. She thought she detected something that upset Stephen at those times, something that made him tighten his lips and study the menu more carefully than was necessary, and she wondered if he didn't like people who weren't born Canadians.

But late at night, the first day Birdie came, she whispered to Stephen, after he'd climbed into bed beside her, whispered, even though the children were asleep and Birdie had left at five to catch the bus that would take her to the subway, that the new woman, Birdie, was not only far from being bird-like in any way, but was also a Negro, he simply asked, his voice loud in the dark room, 'Do you think this one will work out?'

Nadine had nodded to the ceiling. 'I hope so,' she said, still whispering. 'I hope so.'

* * *

Stephen Ladd was an only child who had been christened Stanislaw Ladowski. From the time he started school, Stanislaw was known as Stan, and this lasted until he was twenty-three years old. At that time, he legally changed his name, acquired his real estate licence, and began a new life as Stephen Ladd. By then he had moved far from St. John's Ward, his old neighbourhood, and embraced the new world he had created for himself, easily closing all doors behind him but for one.

It wasn't difficult for Stan to slip the skin of his former life. His father had been a labourer who came to Toronto with his pregnant bride in the second wave of immigrants from Eastern Europe before World War I. A heavyset, brooding man, Stephen's father worked long hours installing the sewer systems that ran beneath the new streets of Toronto. He spoke little and frightened his wife and son with unexplained bouts of rage and monthly drinking episodes that culminated with weeping and praying and begging forgiveness for something that the little boy never understood. He died after suffering a massive stroke when Stan was nine.

Although friendly with everybody, Stan never made any real friends as he was growing up. So when Stanislaw Ladowski more or less disappeared, there was no one left to miss him except his mother. And because of the woman she was, having learned young to say goodbye, she let him go, made no demands on him, held no claims, except for refusing to call him anything but Stasiu.

Mr Stephen Ladd was in the right place at the right time when he chose his career. The post-war boom of building was taking off in Toronto in 1946, and Stephen went with it. Before he was thirty, he had made a small fortune, and had a large staff working under him.

At that time, Stephen's mother passed away, as quietly and with as little bother as she had lived her life. Stephen had been a good son to his small, passive mother, calling her before he left for the office every morning to make sure she was all right, and humouring her by speaking Polish if she was feeling low. When she refused to accept one of the bright, compact apartments that Stephen offered to her, he paid off the remaining mortgage on his dark, narrow, childhood home, and bought her a new fridge and stove. On Sunday afternoons he went back to the old red brick row house, eating his favourite supper of potato and cabbage soup followed by the pork dish he loved so much, the special recipe she always had waiting for him. After they had eaten, Stephen and his mother sat side by side on the plastic-covered couch and listened to the Lux Radio Theatre. Before he left, Stephen would help his mother make sense of any bills or mail she had received during the week. Then he would drive home to his own apartment on the luxurious Oriole Parkway.

* * *

Six months after he buried his mother Stephen began looking for a wife. His mother's death had left a big hole in his life. He had dated sporadically through his adulthood, but didn't seem to need much female companionship. What he did need and miss now was the comfort of knowing he had a real home to go to.

He found Nadine Dixon. Nadine was one of the dozen typists in the big outer office of Ladd Realtors, and was pretty and shiny in the way of a twenty-year-old woman who has left the farm behind and has all her life and its wonderful possibilities stretching out in front of her.

No one was more surprised than Nadine when Stephen first asked her to go out with him. He was her boss, after all, Mr Ladd, the main topic of conversation every morning at coffee time. All the girls whispered and wondered about Mr Ladd; he was so respectful and affable around the typing pool, yet at the same time distant and somehow – unreachable, one of them had said. They reacted to Nadine's news with good-natured jealousy, each of them wondering, to herself, why he would pick Nadine, and not her. Nadine was a bit mousy, they all agreed when she was in the ladies' room, mousy and very unworldly, right off the farm.

But after the first date came a second, and a third, and then Stephen and Nadine were dating regularly. During their courtship the thought briefly crossed Stephen's mind, like a quick sharp stab in a molar that signals trouble, but can be forgotten until it happens the next time, that he should find someone a little more polished than Nadine. Nadine Dixon, who had grown up on a chicken farm near Lindsay, who said things like *Lord love a duck!* when she was shocked by something, and whose biggest wish was to drive all the way north to the shores of Lake Nipissing to see the home of the Dionne quintuplets at Callendar. But for all her naïveté, there was something about Nadine that Stephen couldn't get enough of. There was the way she listened so carefully to everything he said, sometimes murmuring, Gosh! Really? that moved him. There was the unselfconscious quickness of her smile. And the calm way her hands rested in her lap, still and pale, the fingertips just touching, when they went for Sunday drives. Her hands, so untroubled and white, reminded Stephen of two small, ivory shells that he wanted to gather up, tenderly, in his own bigger hands. All these things, Nadine's wonder, her smile, her hands, made him feel taller than he was, taller and somehow smarter. She wasn't one of the modern women he ran into in the business, women who smoked cigarettes and ordered martinis and had loud, confident laughter. Nadine Dixon was a woman who needed to be taken care of.

* * *

Nadine Delores Dixon was the name on Nadine's birth certificate, and when she gave up her maiden name, in May of 1953, she was pleased and proud to be known as Mrs Stephen Ladd.

Shortly before they married, Nadine, at Stephen's suggestion, quit her job at Ladd Realtors. The newlyweds lived in Stephen's apartment for seven months, until Nadine announced, blushing, that she was pregnant, and then they bought a pretty ranch house out in the brand new development of Don Mills. Nadine liked Don Mills, with its curved streets of bungalows and ranch houses, liked bundling their infant daughter Andrea into the carriage and walking the quiet, orderly streets, meeting up with other young mothers and talking about their babies and their decorating plans for their homes and their successful husbands.

When Kevin was born, fourteen months after Andrea, Stephen began talking about moving into Forest Hill, where they would be closer to Upper Canada College, for Kevin, and Bishop Strachan for Andrea. Nadine argued against it, saying she felt safe and comfortable where they were, where sometimes, in the morning, she could look beyond the skeletons of houses under construction and see the mist in the distance, and could almost smell the country air she'd grown up in, and she thought it would be good for the children to be out of the city a little way. But Stephen pointed out that he would be home much more quickly without the forty-minute commute on the Don Valley Parkway.

* * *

And so when Andrea was four and Kevin almost three, the Ladd family moved into the stately manor on Dunvegan Road.

Right from the start, Nadine didn't like Forest Hill. She rarely saw any women her age walking on the streets with children, and the yards were so big and far apart that it was hard to get to know any of her neighbours. She also found the house too big too handle easily. She kept it tidy and clean, but it was a full-time, difficult job with two preschoolers underfoot.

Stephen had immediately hired a gardener to keep up the yard, to plant the flower beds in the spring and cut the grass all summer and do a big fall clean-up of the leaves that fell from the mature silver and Norway maples before winter came. He had hired another man to sweep or shovel any snow that fell on the winding asphalt drive and brick walkway through the coldest months. And he had wanted to get a cleaning lady right away. But Nadine refused. She didn't like to refuse anything to Stephen, but there were some things, in those earlier days of their marriage, that she still insisted on.

Nadine knew all her neighbours had help; she had seen them, women with sloping shoulders under drab cloth coats and low shoes with rundown heels, coming and going on the hushed street in the mornings and then again in the evenings. But Nadine felt that she shouldn't need the help of another woman in her home. It embarrassed her to think about someone washing her family's dirty underwear and scraping crusted food off the plates they had used. Or cleaning her or Stephen's hair out of the bathtub, or worse yet, changing the sheets of their bed. She couldn't bear the thought of another woman knowing those intimate details of her life, and maybe thinking she was dirty, or lazy, or spoiled.

She knew Stephen wouldn't be able to understand her feelings about such details, so she just shook her head, and said no, I can manage, until he left her alone about it.

Things got a little easier for Nadine when both children were in school. She made a weekly plan of her household chores, and if she got started on the cleaning and laundry right after she dropped the children off at nine o'clock, she could be sure to have most things in order by the time she picked them up again at three-thirty. She would feed them by five, and have them in bed before Stephen arrived home, sometimes at eight, sometimes at nine. Then they would have their dinner together at the gleaming rosewood table in the dining room, by candlelight, with a bottle of the aged wine Stephen ordered from the Opimian Society, which he had joined shortly after moving into Forest Hill.

Stephen would call her if he was grabbing a bite out due to a late showing, and those evenings Nadine would eat her supper with the children, and then sit in the den, reading the book she had taken from the library on her Friday morning visit, or watching one of the silly sitcoms that had started appearing on evening television.

And so the years passed for Nadine, serenely and with little discord. But as the children grew older, she would sometimes wonder, as she stopped the dust cloth in the middle of a windowsill to gaze out the window at the scudding grey clouds bringing soft rains, and realize that another spring was upon them, if this was all there was. At times like those, which seemed to come closer and closer together, she found it harder and harder to stay quiet and still on the outside, when she felt loud and jumpy inside. It seemed to be everywhere, this loudness, in her skull, through her chest, even in her hands and feet. It would take her a while, but when she finally settled herself down, she would be filled with some great sadness, and feel the urge to do something silly, something unpredictable, maybe even a little rude. But then she would give herself a good shake, and make herself think more sensibly.

'Whatever is wrong with me?' she would ask, forcing

herself to remember the less fortunate women she read about in the newspaper, or saw on the six o'clock news. Women who had husbands who beat them, who left them penniless with small children. Women who had to get up in the dark and drop their children off at a babysitter and work all day, on their feet, to come home in the dark again and cook a pot of macaroni for supper.

'You are one of the lucky ones, Nadine Ladd,' she would tell herself. She had attained her dream, after all, the dream of so many young women growing up in the thirties and forties in the Ontario countryside, or in countrysides all over North America, the dream of a good husband and healthy children and a beautiful home. She had attained her dream, and so how could she dare to ask for anything more?

She thought about her sisters, Joan out west, living in the Okanagan, and Lorraine, still back in Lindsay. Neither of them had been as successful as Nadine. The three girls hadn't been very close when they were young, and had failed to grow into the closeness that often comes when sisters reach adulthood. They wrote to each other occasionally, and Nadine felt that she could read a lot of unhappiness between the lines of those few-and-far-between letters.

Joan's husband had taken to drinking when he'd had some bad luck with losing two jobs in one year, and Lorraine had never married, and still lived on the chicken farm with their aging parents, although by now the chickens had been sold. Lorraine's income as a schoolteacher in town supplemented Mr and Mrs Dixon's old age pensions, and every Christmas Nadine, after first checking with Stephen, sent a generous cheque home to the farm. She always received a letter from Lorraine, and another from her mother, by the first week in January, reporting what the money would be used for – one year a new roof on the house, another year new tires for the car, new dentures or eyeglasses or prescription pills, and, a few years ago, a double burial plot in the Twin Oaks Cemetery in Lindsay. This expenditure had been the one that seemed the most exciting to Nadine's parents, and Nadine's mother had written, at quite a bit of length compared to her usual brief thank-you, on the placement of the plot, and even enclosed a brochure showing an illustration of the styles of granite headstones from which they could choose.

Whenever Nadine thought about the farm, and the strutting, aloof chickens, she told herself she was glad that she, unlike Lorraine, had been able to get away. But when she remembered all those quiet hours she had spent candling the eggs after school and on weekends, a kind of tranquillity descended on her. She had liked egg candling, although she never admitted it. Her sisters had hated it, and weren't good at it; they were slow and unlike Nadine they broke eggs.

Nadine's mother had candled eggs eight hours a day, five days a week. Their farm had more than three thousand chickens, and the full-time production, supplying hundreds of eggs every week to the CNR for their dining car, gave them enough money to get by on. Nadine's father and mother ran the farm single-handed, although the girls were expected to do their share. Since Nadine was a faster, more careful candler, she worked alongside her mother after school while Joan and Lorraine got the supper on. On Saturdays, when her mother and father went into Lindsay to get groceries, the other two girls did the housework and laundry, while Nadine headed out to the chicken houses to collect as many eggs as she could handle that day, gently clean them with the fine sandpaper brush, pile them into galvanized pails, then carry them back into the house, into the small room off the kitchen where she would sit for six hours at a stretch. Some Saturdays she could do fifteen pails, checking the eggs, grading them, and filling stack after stack of the cardboard crates that each held two and a half dozen eggs.

Nadine remembered the smooth feel of the eggs, the easy way her wrist could give a quick, firm turn as she held the egg in front of the light in the candling box, showing her the yolk spinning on its chalazas. Whenever a hairline crack was visible in the light, or a spot showed up on a yolk, she put that egg in a separate pail, for their own use in the house. The tiny imperfections, caused by who knew what, meant the egg wasn't good for table use by the CNR. But they didn't bother any of the Dixons when the eggs were stirred and beaten and whipped into cakes and puddings and biscuits and soups.

There had been something soothing for Nadine in the quiet monotony of the candling room. She had passed hundreds and hundreds, thousands, of eggs in front of her young eyes, making up stories about being discovered by a talent scout as she stood in one of the aisles of Harwell's General Store in Lindsay, about becoming a figure skater who performed more leaps and twirls than even Barbara Ann Scott, about being married to a handsome man and having two children, a girl and a boy, and living in a fancy house in Toronto.

* * *

Nadine's father died of cardiac arrest in the bitterness of a cold snap that hovered over Ontario for much of that February of 1968. After the funeral, Lorraine told Nadine and Joan that when their mother felt a little better, a little stronger, they would discuss selling the farm. There was no need to keep it any longer, Lorraine said, it was only their father who had loved it, after all. And wasn't it a blessing that he had finally paid off the mortgage the year before? A blessing because that had been his only real goal in life, to own his own land, free and clear. Yes, it was only Dad who had really loved the place, Lorraine said, Joan nodding in agreement.

Nadine said nothing, looking out the kitchen window at the blackened, gnarled trunk of the huge old oak that stood to one side of the yard. Later, while the funeral guests were eating the lunch she and her sisters had prepared and put out, she went to the egg candling room and shut the door behind her. It was used for storage now, piled with broken wooden furniture that Archie Dixon had always meant to get around to repairing, and stacks of damp-looking cardboard boxes filled with whatever it was her mother couldn't part with, old clothes and knick-knacks and musty magazines and, in one corner, the artificial silver Christmas tree Lorraine had bought that year.

The stool that Nadine had perched on, all those hours and days and years that she worked on the eggs, was still there, and Nadine ran her palm over the smooth seat, wiping off the dust. Then she sat down on it, with her hands resting quietly in her lap, resting more quietly than they had in a long time. Nadine sat until her feet began to grow cold and she knew she should go back in and do her share of the washing up.

* * *

Stephen finally insisted on having someone in, as he described it, to help out, a few months after they had buried Nadine's father. He asked Nadine, rather gruffly, as they were driving to the O'Keefe Centre through a warm, windy pink May evening, if she was having trouble coping. Without waiting for her answer, he went on to ask if this trouble she was having was because of her father's death. Stephen cleared his throat a number of times while he asked these unanswered questions, glancing at himself in the rear-view mirror. Because things had seemed different with her, with Nadine, for quite a while now, he went on, but maybe it was old Archie passing that had made Nadine even less able to run things. It wasn't anything in particular, Stephen said, it was just that he had noticed, over the last year, and especially in the last few months, that the house was less than sparkling clean. Dishes always piled in the sink, wet towels on the bathroom floor, and some days he would have to wear the same shirt he'd worn the day before, because Nadine hadn't done the ironing. And the children, well, the children were another matter.

Nadine had listened quietly while he talked about the house, but it was what he had to say about the children that made her eyes fill. He said he thought that she had really fallen down on the job with the children, fifteen-year-old Andrea and fourteen-year-old Kevin.

They were spoiled and unruly teenagers, he said, and he'd frequently heard them talking back to their mother. They made a mess of the house, always had music or the television blaring, brought their friends in at all hours, and just seemed to make life quite unpleasant in a number of ways. Kevin had refused, he pointed out, refused to get a haircut for over three months now, and the school had phoned him at the office to complain. And Andrea was looking very – straggly, somehow. She no longer curled her long strawberry-blonde hair, and it looked thin and limp. As soon as she got home from school she changed out of her uniform and into ridiculous outfits, jeans with huge wide pant legs and off-the-shoulder gypsy blouses and fringed vests. Stephen didn't want to look too closely, but he suspected, he said in a sudden urgent whisper, even though they were alone in the car, that Andrea had stopped wearing a brassiere. Had Nadine even noticed? Really, she'd better talk to the girl before she got herself into trouble.

Nadine, rummaging in her purse for a tissue to wipe her nose, had nodded. Nodded about Andrea and her lack of a bra, about Andrea and Kevin in general, about the house, and yes, finally yes, she nodded, turning her head away, looking at the traffic beside them on Yonge Street as they drew up to the O'Keefe Centre, yes about a cleaning lady, too.

She knew it was kind of Stephen to be concerned about the house, really, she knew that most women would be grateful for a husband who wanted to make life easier, who said that all the work was too hard on her. It was kind of him, but still, it was an embarrassment, wasn't it, to have to admit that you were too weak to look after your own family?

She knew they wanted it to be like it used to, when she had been up before all of them, cooking them a proper breakfast, having their lunches made and waiting on the counter, smiling as they went out the door and smiling when they came back in again, as if she hadn't moved all day. They liked the savoury smells of expensive cuts of cooking meat funnelling down the hall toward them as soon as they opened the door; they liked the lemon polish that hinted of well-being wafting from the dining room and its lustrous wood, they even liked the acrid, assuring smell of bleach in the bathroom.

But she couldn't do it now; she tried, Lord knows she tried, but it was as if her bones had lost their sturdy marrow and were instead filled with some thin, stringy substance that didn't let her move properly, kept her from getting up in the morning, kept her from her automatic propelling through the house, stooping and lifting and pushing and pulling and chopping and peeling. The stretchy feeling even filled her skull cavity, with the strange sensation of crowding her brain, so that her thinking was fuzzy, and she had to concentrate to remember what she'd had for lunch, or if she had eaten at all. It kept her from feeling rushed, from worrying over the children's behaviour, from thinking about how long it was since she and Stephen had even touched each other, and while that was a comfort, not worrying any more, at the same time, she was plagued by a vague sense of unease, as if there was something she was forgetting to do.

Of course, Nadine went to the doctor. She wasn't a fool; like Stephen, she too wondered exactly what her problem was. She knew it wasn't anything to do with her father's death. He hadn't affected her much when he was alive, and affected her less dead. But she didn't want to tell Stephen that, thought it better if he attributed some of her unfamiliar behaviour to mourning.

She was given a clean bill of health, told, by first one doctor, then another, that she was physically in good shape, although a bit underweight, and as for her complaints about not being able to get a good hold on things, up here, the doctor had said, tapping his temple the way Nadine had when she'd been talking about her feelings, well, as for that, the first doctor recommended a vacation. The second suggested getting out of the house, maybe taking an evening course in macramé or Chinese cooking offered at the local high school, perhaps even – what had she done before she was married – oh, egg candling and then typing – perhaps some sort of office job.

Nadine listened seriously to these men, as she always listened to men, and did consider both options. She couldn't think of any place she'd like to go on a holiday, then thought about going out to visit Joan – she had always been a bit closer to Joan, and they hadn't seen each other, except for the funeral, since Kevin was eight or nine. She went so far as to call about flight schedules and fees, and left the information written on the note pad beside the phone in her bedroom.

She looked through the paper, eyeing the classifieds, but all of the job descriptions frightened her, made her realize that she could never take on the huge responsibility of getting the old manual typewriter out of the basement and seeing if she still remembered where to put her fingers, to say nothing of buying a new wardrobe to wear to work, and then the worries over the dark mornings and evenings in the winter, and unlit parking lots, the income tax forms that would start arriving in the mail, and what if something happened to Andrea or Kevin, one of those school accidents, a jammed thumb during volley-ball practice, a sudden high fever during math class, and she wasn't home when the school phoned to ask her to come and pick up either one or the other. No. Nadine closed the paper, folding it back to its original shape, and surveyed the mess in the kitchen from the night before, when Andrea and two of her girlfriends had been snacking as they did their homework together at the table.

Then she opened the phonebook to the yellow pages, studying the listing of employment agencies.

* * *

Nadine secretly watches Birdie. She studies the woman's thick arms, her crown of coarse hair, the hard high mound of her buttocks moving under the clean cotton dress. Nadine admires the woman's physical strength as she catches a glimpse of her moving a heavy armchair so she can vacuum under it, is envious of the apparent tirelessness of the large, rounded calves as they climb the stairs, quickly, time after time.

Nadine has forgotten what it feels like to move with such fluid ease, even though her body feels full of water.

It is a month later, the middle of October, when the agency calls Nadine. They are doing a first-month check on their employee, they tell her, and wonder if there are any problems.

'No,' Nadine tells the brisk voice on the other end of the line. 'No, Birdie is a very hard worker. She's always on time, and hasn't missed a day yet. And she's very pleasant,' Nadine adds, for a reason she doesn't know, and not quite truthfully. It isn't that Birdie is rude, or sullen. It's just that Nadine can't read her, understand what she thinks about anything, about the house, or the job, or about her, Nadine.

'I'm glad to hear all that,' the agency woman says. 'Unfortunately, we're having a small problem with Birdie here at our end.'

Nadine frowns, putting her index finger into the first circle of the telephone's rotary dial, and moving the finger around and around, slowly.

'The people she lives with have just brought over more family members, and they have asked Birdie to move out,' the woman explains, while Nadine's finger stops on the number three. 'It was a temporary arrangement for the last year,' the woman continues. 'Birdie knew it wasn't permanent. But she has to find a place of her own now.'

Nadine makes a polite, interested noise in her throat, wondering how this involves her, how it affects Birdie coming to work for her.

'I'm just letting you know,' the woman says patiently, 'that Birdie's application indicates that she would like to live in.'

When she realizes it is her turn to speak, Nadine thinks about the last statement, then asks, 'Live in what?'

There is a second of silence. 'Live in with the employer,' the woman answers. Is there less patience in her voice now? 'Some nannies and housekeepers live out, on their own, and some live in, with certain days away, staying with relatives or whatever. Some prefer Tuesday afternoon and Sunday off, some Saturday morning and Sunday, usually whatever is best for the employer. I'm just mentioning this to you because I wanted you to have first say. Birdie will have to find a place of her own if you don't want her. If she has to move too far away, or some place where the bus and subway connections are too complicated, we may place her somewhere else. But I'm quite sure she can find another woman that she can share accommodations with; actually, I have a list on file. A list of women who need to share their rent. I can let Birdie have a look at it. But if you're at all interested in having her live in – well, you actually save money, because of course the salary decreases, once they're given their board and room.'

Nadine reaches the o on the dial by this point. 'I'll have to discuss this with my family,' she says.

'Of course,' the woman answers. 'But Birdie will need to know in the next two weeks. Oh,' the woman says, as if she just remembered, 'she told me that she's quite happy working for you.'

Nadine is surprised at the small, shivering surge of joy she feels. 'She is?'

'Yes.'

'It's just that she never says much,' Nadine says. 'And she doesn't smile, either. So I wasn't sure ...'

'That is just the way of many of our employees, Mrs Ladd. Some of these women don't have much to smile about.' There is a tone in the woman's voice Nadine can't quite recognize. 'So you'll let me know about the living in?'

'Yes. Yes, I'll call you.'

Nadine hangs up the phone and stays at the telephone table in the short hall between the kitchen and the foyer. She hears a distant rhythmic hum, and listens, thinking it is the intimate sound of her own blood coursing through her veins. She realizes, after ten, or maybe twenty seconds, that it is Birdie, vacuuming one of the upstairs bedrooms.

* * *

Nadine, in an odd moment of what is, for her, defiance, does not ask Stephen's opinion, does not gently break it to the children that their home is about to change, will now house another body.

And so, a week after the phone call, Birdie stands in the foyer, at her usual time of eight-thirty, with one battered brown suitcase and a well-used Eaton shopping bag.

'You can take as long as you need, Birdie,' Nadine says, smiling, 'to get yourself settled. Will the bedroom be all right? Will you have enough room for everything?' She lets her eyes drop to the suitcase and bag, and bites the inside of her cheek, realizing that even though the bedroom is small, there is obviously more than enough room for Birdie's few possessions.

'Plenty of room, Missus. There be plenty of room for me and my things,' Birdie says. She looks into Nadine's eyes as she says this. Nadine is confused, almost embarrassed, at this unfamiliar but somehow significant moment. Birdie has never before looked into her employer's face, but has kept her eyes fixed on the floor or on some piece of Nadine's clothing when Nadine gives her instructions.

When Andrea comes home, later than usual that day because she had a detention at school, she encounters Birdie coming out of the bathroom between her bedroom and the guest room. She doesn't say anything to Birdie – the truth is, she has never spoken to Birdie, except once, to tell her to please not touch anything in her room, just pick up the clothes and put them on the bed. Now Andrea goes downstairs to find her mother.

'Why's she still here?' Andrea asks Nadine, who is sitting in the small solarium off the dining room. 'Did she miss her bus?'

'No,' Nadine says. 'She's staying here now.'

'What do you mean, staying here?' Andrea picks up a long strand of her hair from beside her face, divides it into three sections, and starts to braid it.

'She's staying. Living here,' Nadine answers.

Andrea drops the hair. 'LIVING here?'

'Yes,' Nadine says, running her fingertip up and down one broad dustless leaf of the huge *Ficus benjamina* that hangs over the cushioned white wicker chair she sits in. She stops at the tip of the leaf, noticing that it is turning brown. 'I'm giving this too much water,' she says, not that Andrea is interested. Even when Nadine is alone in the solarium she talks out loud;

she has read that plants respond to the sound of the human voice, to music.

'She can't just move in here,' Andrea says, her mouth turning down at the corners.

'She has,' Nadine says.

'Mother!'

At the girl's exasperated tone, Nadine looks away from the leaf, up to her daughter, who is still standing in front of her.

'Yes?'

'Are you nuts? We don't need some ... some ...,' Andrea searches for the word, 'some PERSON, just coming in here and living with us. I mean, she can clean the house, sure, but why does she have to LIVE here? And what does Daddy say about it?' She says the last sentence even more quickly than the rest, as if she has just thought of it, and realizes it is her trump card.

Nadine leans her head against the flowered cushion behind her. She keeps looking at her daughter, seeing the dark eyeliner around her eyes, how it makes her blue eyes stand out in her pale face. Huge and startled-looking, her eyes made up with silver eyeshadow, dark blue eyeliner on the edge of her top and bottom eyelids, and black, black mascara on her lashes. Only eye make-up, Nadine thinks, and so much. No colour on her cheeks or lips. When did she start doing this? Why haven't I noticed before? Does she think she looks attractive? Is this the style? All these questions fill Nadine's mind.

'Well?' Andrea says. 'What does Daddy say?'

Nadine gets up. 'He wants me to have help around the house,' she says, facing her daughter.

Andrea shrugs, her shoulders twitching angrily. 'Why? You never needed help before.'

Nadine suddenly wonders if the girl is eating properly. Looking more closely, she sees that Andrea's cheeks are quite hollow. 'We're having lamb for dinner,' she says. 'Do you like lamb?' She can't remember if it is Andrea or Kevin who always kicks up a fuss when they have lamb, but she knows that one of them won't eat it.

* * *

One evening in early December, Nadine knocks softly on Birdie's door. She hears a murmur that she takes for come in, and opens the door. The room is in darkness, but in the light from the hall she sees Birdie standing by the window, looking out. She turns as Nadine enters the room.

Nadine can't make out Birdie's face; she feels for the light switch, flips it up.

'Birdie,' Nadine says, 'why are you in the dark? What are you doing, just standing there?'

Birdie's eyes are on Nadine's waist. 'You want I should mind the children, Missus? You and the Mister would like to be going out?'

'No. I told you, Birdie, you don't have to baby-sit. They're old enough to be on their own. No. I just meant ... maybe you'd like to watch television.'

'Oh, no, thank you, Missus.' There is a polite smile on Birdie's lips. There are deep lines on either side of her mouth.

Nadine looks around the room. 'Well,' she says. She looks at the string of rosary beads hanging on a tack over Birdie's bed. The top of the bedside table holds a plastic alarm clock, bright orange, and a small metal goose-necked reading lamp. The chest of drawers wears its usual starched white cutwork runner. On top of the runner sits a glass of water and a plate, one of the kitchen plates, and on it is piece of buttered toast and a hard-boiled egg. There is a plain wooden chair on one side of the chest of drawers.

Nadine knows everything in the room, except the rosary and the clock.

'Would you like something to read?' she asks Birdie. She knows Birdie can read, has seen her reading the labels on cans, the instructions on bottles of cleaning spray, a bus schedule. 'A book? Or a magazine? I've got all kinds of magazines.' Nadine tries not to stare at the egg.

'No, thank you, Missus.'

'Are you sure?' Nadine clears her throat. 'Wouldn't you like ... something to do?'

Birdie keeps her gaze on the belt around Nadine's waist, the thin brown snakeskin belt with the heavy gold buckle that Nadine wears with her tan wool slacks. The smile is still there, polite, fixed in place. Thirty seconds pass. Nadine feels a stickiness in her armpits.

'I could clean that silver again, Missus.'

'No. I ... I just meant – well, I thought you might want something, something of your own, to do.'

Birdie's smile becomes wider. 'Oh, Missus. Don't worry about Birdie. See, I do something.' She waves a hand toward the window.

The younger woman looks toward the glass pane. The snowflakes softly fall towards the beckoning death of the spotlights under the carefully tended branches of Prince of Wales juniper at the back of the house.

'But it's dark, Birdie. And there's nothing out there, in the yard. What are you looking at?'

A furrow appears between Birdie's thick, greying eyebrows. 'The snow, Missus. I look at the snow, listen to it.'

Nadine turns the rings on her left hand around and around with her right hand, runs her fingers over the cluster of diamonds. 'Well, if you're sure you're ... all right. Don't need anything.'

The smile is different now. 'No, Missus.'

Nadine leans her head forward; Birdie's voice is that low.

'I'm not needing anything. Not one thing at all.'

Nadine abruptly looks down, as if she'd discovered something new, or missing, on her ring. She raises her head, her lips firm. 'Good night then, Birdie.'

She puts her hand on the doorknob, then turns around to face Birdie again. 'Is that all you're having for supper, Birdie? Just an egg and toast?' she says. She has never witnessed Birdie eating anything. She knows Birdie must eat, couldn't work the way she does and keep up her size without eating a fair amount, but still, she has never seen her eat. The first day that Birdie lived with them, Nadine asked her if she'd like to eat her dinner with them, at the dining-room table. Birdie looked at the top of Nadine's head. Nadine thought she saw something new in Birdie's eyes, something, could it be laughter? 'Oh, no, Missus. Oh no. Thank you, Missus,' Birdie said, as politely as always.

'You just take whatever you want then, Birdie. Please make sure you take what you want,' Nadine repeated, not sure what was proper etiquette for live-in help and their meals. She hoped she hadn't somehow offended Birdie; on the other hand, she hoped she hadn't made a fool of herself, inviting Birdie to eat with them.

Now Birdie looks toward the egg. 'I like an egg, now and again, for my evening meal, Missus.'

Nadine walks to the chest of drawers, looks more closely at the egg, as if there is something about it she doesn't understand. Birdie is still standing by the bed.

Nadine reaches her fingers toward it, and then, with no warning, picks it up. It is still warm. She runs her palms over the smoothness of the shell, then suddenly holds it up toward the ceiling, between her face and the light fixture.

'I used to do this,' she says. When Birdie doesn't respond, Nadine continues. 'I used to do this, when I was a girl. Look inside eggs. I'd hold them in front of a light, and look inside, make sure everything was as it was supposed to be. It's called egg candling, because before there was electricity people held the eggs in front of a candle.' She looks at Birdie. 'Of course, you can't do it with a boiled egg.'

Birdie is looking at the egg in Nadine's hands.

Nadine reaches up and sets it back on the plate. 'Well, good night, Birdie,' she says, not moving.

'Good night, Missus. Thank you, Missus,' Birdie says, as she concludes every conversation with Nadine, even when Nadine simply tells her not to wash Mr Ladd's green sweater in hot water. Nadine always wonders what Birdie is thanking her for.

She leaves Birdie, clicking the door behind her. She stands in the upstairs hall, listening to the whirring rush of the dishwasher in the kitchen, the roar of television laughter from somewhere in the house, a heavy bass beat from Kevin's room down the hall, and Stephen's voice, loud, argumentative, on the phone in the den beside the foyer.

She looks back at Birdie's closed door, and at that moment sees the thin rim of light under the door disappear, and she has to put her hand up, over her mouth.

While she still has her hand up, the door opens again, just a crack at first, then wider.

'I think you would like to come back in, Missus.' Birdie says. Her voice is even lower than it was in the bedroom, a minute earlier, if that is possible.

Nadine puts her hand down, blinking her eyes rapidly. She nods, then goes into Birdie's room, and shuts the door behind her. She stands, awkwardly, like she is the visitor, the one who doesn't really live here, while Birdie turns on the gooseneck lamp beside the bed, then goes to the window and looks out again.

'Sit down, Missus, please,' she says, to her own reflection in the glass.

Nadine sits on the edge of the bed, working her fingers together. She asks the question that's been on her mind since she first saw Birdie, standing on the front step. 'Is Birdie your real name?'

The other woman turns to face her. 'No,' she says. 'But seem like Birdie fit me more better.'

Nadine has to force her lips to stay together. She tells herself, Wait, wait, Nadine, having learned, finally, how many times her quick, light voice and unimportant questions have stopped people from telling her the important things.

Birdie walks to the chair beside the chest of drawers and lowers herself, with surprising gracefulness, onto the hard wooden seat. Her back is straight, her breasts enormous, straining at the thin cotton of her dress, pulling the buttons apart.

Nadine wonders what it is that is so odd-looking about Birdie, until she realizes she has never before seen Birdie sitting down. Actually, she has rarely seen Birdie straight on.

She is usually looking at Birdie's back – as the woman stands at the kitchen counter, or curves over the surfaces she is dusting or polishing or wiping, or bends over the hose of the vacuum as she pushes and pulls it with no apparent effort.

So now she waits, waits to hear the story of Birdie's name. She knows Birdie is about to tell her a story, can feel it in the room with them, the story coming. And she doesn't know how she knows this, she was never told any stories when she was a child, but she can just feel it in the air.

'Birdie the name my old granny call me, back in Trinidad,' Birdie says at that very moment, as if she, too, knew the time was right, knew Nadine was now ready to listen.

'Trinidad,' Nadine says, nodding in surprise. She hadn't thought of Trinidad, but now it makes perfect sense.

'There is a story some people know. About a little bird who grows big,' Birdie says. She shifts on the chair, and licks her lips. Watching her, Nadine thinks, with mild surprise, that perhaps Birdie isn't as old as she first thought.

Nadine nods, releasing her shoulders and crossing her ankles, letting her hands uncurl in her lap.

'This is what happened,' Birdie says, and she tells this story:

There was a child, a small boy, whose mother had died. His father married himself another woman, as men do. The woman didn't like the child, was mean to him, oh, she buffed him good. She left his clothes all in tatters, never gave him enough to eat. But this boy was a good, happy boy. Sometimes he cry when the troubles felt too big, but then he would stop, and smile. He was that good a boy.

The meanest thing was, this woman had many bags of food she keep in the storeroom behind the kitchen. But she never give any to the boy, she keep it to sell at market.

One day, the boy walk along the road. In the middle of the road he see a little bird, hopping here, hopping there. The boy pick up the bird, and put her in his pocket. At home, he sat the little bird down on the floor in front of the kitchen door, and he start to sing to it. But the bird, she sing nothing. The boy stroke her, and give her little pieces he keep from his own sorry food, and whistle to her.

When the bird hear this whistle, she perk right up and start to whistle back. That bird sure can whistle; she whistle so loud, and all of a sudden she burst into song. She sing one beautiful tune after another. She sing so loud that the mean old stepmother, she come stomping out the door to hear what makes such a noise.

But this mean woman, she couldn't hear the beauty of the song, because she just not made that way. Instead, she shout, 'You there! Lazy bad boy! What is this noise?'

The boy be all surprised. 'Mother,' he say, 'don't be angry. Look, look at the little bird I find on the road. Listen to her beautiful songs.'

But the stepmother just look at that little bird. 'You know there are too many lazy people in the house that I have to look after all the time,' she say. 'Even you, you boy, are all by yourself too much for me.' She walk close to the bird, her hands on her hips, and look down at it. 'And that lazy little bird, why, if she were bigger I would twist it neck and eat it!'

At these words the bird, she stop. She look right in the eye of the woman. Well, I tell you now, the woman, she get might afraid when she see how that bird look at her. The bird sing out to the woman, 'Food, give me food.'

The woman shook her head. 'See, boy, that's what I tell you. You always causing trouble. First you want food, and now you bring home this damned bird, making noise on my head, asking for food!'

At this, the little bird flew around in circles over the woman's head, shrieking out her song for food, and swooping down on the woman.

The woman covered her head, crying, and said to the boy, 'Look, look! This bird be the Devil, trying to pluck out my eyes and bring me bad luck. Run, run boy, to the pantry and bring a bag of rice to her, to make her stop her song.'

The boy brought the big bag of rice, that bag be twenty pounds or more, and with one stroke of her little beak, the bird opened the bag wide open. She pecked and pecked and pecked, and in a few minutes nothing was left. She grew as big as a hen, with a shining coat, turned all beautiful colours. Oh, you should see the beauty of this bird! Her wings were blue powdered with yellow, the likes of nothing the boy and his stepmother ever seen.

The bird now opened her beak very wide and sang, 'Food, give me food.'

The stepmother started to grumble at the boy again, complaining about him bringing home this bird who wanted to eat up all her food, but the bird, so much bigger, started her swooping, her wings way out wide.

The woman yelled to the boy, 'Run to the granary and get all the sorghum you can find. If that doesn't work, than surely, we will be eaten up!'

The boy obeyed, and ran back with seven bags of sorghum.

'Watch me eat!' the bird sang, its song now frightening.

The woman screamed to God for help, but the bird shrieked and told her to shut up.

That bird crushed the grain like a mill. The more she ate, the bigger she grew. By the time she had finished the seven bags of sorghum, she was taller than the boy. She flapped her wings and made such a wind that the boy and his stepmother could hardly find their breath.

At that time the boy's father started to come toward the house. The woman cried to her husband, 'Quick, man. Bring your machete to the kitchen!'

But the man couldn't hear over the rush of the wings. He came inside, and went to his wife. The wife whispered to him to choke the bird, but the bird heard her words, and swooped down on her.

Fearing for her life, the woman cried to the bird, 'I am begging your pardon, please, please bird, what I have is yours. Take all I have.' Then she turned to the crying boy and said, 'Go! Go now, and bring everything we have.'

The boy came back with seven bags of maize. By now, each wing of the bird was as heavy as a five-pound can, and still, she was growing all the time. When she finished the maize, her head reached the top of the house, she shook her wings, and the whole house shook with it and she still sang, her voice like thunder, she sang to the woman for more food.

'We have no more,' the woman screamed. Then she looked at the boy, and pointed. 'Eat him, eat him! He's the one who brought you here.'

The bird looked at the woman's pointing finger, and the weeping little boy. Then she looked back at the woman and opened her mouth. The woman went to that beak like a butterfly that goes to the sun, and the bird swallowed her up. Then the bird looked at the father. The father ran at her with his machete, but the bird swallowed him whole.

The child was so scared now, and he threw himself flat on the ground and caught the bird's wing and kissed it, begging, 'Bird, he is my father! Please, bird, give me back my father! He is a good man!'

The bird stopped its noise and flapping, and looked down on the little boy.

'You are a good child,' she sang, softer now, 'so I will give you back your father. But promise me you will take me back to where you found me.'

Then she spat out the father, and made her body smaller and smaller, until she was once more the quiet little bird. 'Now take me back to the middle of the road,' she said to the boy.

And so he did.

* * *

Nadine is stretched out on the bed, her head resting against the pillow. When Birdie's voice stops, she sits up.

'Were you like that little bird?' she asks.

Birdie chuckles, a deep, surprising sound. 'When I was born, Missus, you wouldn't believe it. I be no bigger than that.' She puts her little finger up in the air. 'Everyone, my mother, granny, my aunts, everyone try to make me bigger. But I don't want to eat. I don't make a sound. They think for sure I die.

Then one day, when I sleep outside, under the breadfruit tree, a big old noisy bird fly over. He make a loud, loud squawk. My granny, who sit and watch me, see me open my eyes. I start to cry about that squawk, and I cry and cry. Then my granny try to feed me, and this time I take the food. I take more and more, and then I scream and cry for more food. Everybody come to see that skinny old baby eating and eating. Well, I don't stop, Missus. After that day I want food all the time, and when I'm only six years old I'm as big as my granny, and when I'm eight I'm as big as my mother, and when ten I'm as big as my uncle, and I keep eating and growing. So my granny always tell that story to me, about the little bird who grows. And from that first day I start to cry, my mouth open like a bird, waiting for food, everyone calls me Birdie.'

Nadine smiles, and nods, and when Birdie stands up, Nadine does, too, and goes to the door, still smiling.

'Good night, Birdie,' she says, for the third time, then adds, 'thank you.'

'Good night now, Missus,' Birdie answers.

* * *

Nadine is looking for a box of pictures she knows is in one of the storage closets in the basement. The box holds mostly pictures of Andrea and Kevin when they were babies and then toddlers and then off to school, pictures of Andrea in tap-dancing shoes and in a Brownie uniform and sitting astride a horse, pictures of Kevin holding up his swimming badges and in a football jersey and pictures of both of them wearing ice skates and skis and bathing suits. There are a few older pictures, too, pictures of her own younger life, her life on the farm, and it is these pictures she is looking for.

She goes down the narrow stairs and toward the row of closet doors, but catches a glimpse of Birdie in the furnace room, which also houses the washer and dryer. As usual, Birdie has her back to the door. She is ironing. Nadine watches, silently, as Birdie finishes another of Stephen's white shirts, glides it onto a hanger, and slips the hanger onto one of the wire clotheslines that run back and forth across the ceiling of the furnace room.

Nadine sees Birdie's bare legs; she never wears stockings, only ankle socks, white ankle socks and soft beige canvas shoes. Nadine looks at the smooth dark marble of Birdie's calves, like columns, like tree trunks, unmoving, growing up from the cement basement floor. She hears the thump of the iron, smells the hot, sweet smell of starch and clean cotton. At the sudden brash bleat of the dryer, both women start. Birdie leaves the iron and goes to the dryer, opening the door and piling a mound of white sheets into a plastic laundry basket at her feet.

Nadine hesitates a moment, then goes into the furnace room. Birdie looks up at Nadine as she is shaking one sheet free from the tangle in the basket. Nadine catches hold of one of the dangling ends, and grabs the second end and, without speaking, the two women give the sheet a gigantic shake and then another, in the perfect, practised rhythm that all women seem to possess when it comes to sheets. The sheet billows and rises between them, up and up in a huge white oval, and then slowly deflates.

'Tell me about Trinidad, Birdie,' Nadine says. 'Did you have your own home? Do you have children?'

Birdie takes the end of the sheet from Nadine, and folds it up against the huge shelf of her bosom. 'Oh yes, Missus. I had my own house, and I have me four sweet children. All grown up now.' She bends and pulls another sheet out of the basket. 'Oh, I sure do miss their craziness, Missus. Those children, the way they could lime.'

Nadine takes her end of the sheet again. 'Lime?'

Birdie laughs now. Out loud. 'Play. Have fun. Don't do their work if they can hide from me. All young peoples does lime. It's just their way, Missus.' In spite of the laughter, there is a heaviness in Birdie's voice. 'Maybe some of them come here, to Canada, by and by.'

'Tell me about them, Birdie,' Nadine says, and settles her

back against the dryer, against the hot metal front of the dryer, as she helps Birdie fold the laundry.

* * *

Although the weather is still wintry, there is the promise of some lightness, something in the air, when Nadine brings up the idea she has been thinking about, dreaming about, that has been growing in her mind, steadily.

'I phoned Lorraine the other day,' she tells her husband in bed. This is the only time they talk; after the house is quiet and in darkness. Or rather, this is the only time Nadine talks to Stephen. Stephen, Nadine has noticed for the last few years, doesn't have a specific time for talking to Nadine. He usually tells her things as he remembers them, like 'Hornsby finally sold that apartment tower he's had for over a year,' or 'There's no brown shoe polish,' or 'We're invited for drinks at Tim and Susan's on the twenty-sixth,' but Nadine doesn't consider this talking.

'She had to take Mom to the doctor, that specialist, all the way over to Peterborough; she's got a cataract in the other eye, now.'

Stephen sighs.

'She says they're all set for the move into town next week. They've left a lot of the furniture in the house at the farm. They don't need much for the new place; it's a lot smaller. Lorraine says they decided to wait until summer before they try to put the farm up for sale.' Nadine stops, then continues. 'I told her not to do anything about the farm without talking to me first.' She waits again.

Finally Stephen speaks. 'Why?'

Nadine closes her eyes, opens them again. She can just make out the shadow of the light fixture on the ceiling over the bed. 'I've been thinking about the farm a lot lately. Maybe it would be good for the kids to spend some time out there. This summer. Instead of going to camp, I could drive them to the farm, and –'

'Don't be ridiculous, Nadine,' Stephen says. 'Can you really see either of them there, in the heat and flies, miles away from anything? They'd be bored stiff in a day.'

'I think it would be good for them. Away from here for a while. Away from their friends. And you could come out for a week or so – ' She stops as Stephen turns over, his back to her.

'Let Lorraine sell it,' he says. 'You'll never catch me going out to that godforsaken place.'

And soon his breathing is deep and even, but Nadine stays awake for a long time, focusing on the pale white shadow of the light fixture.

* * *

A few weeks later Stephen does something he never does. He comes home early. There had been an office party over the noon hour, a going-away lunch for one of the stenos who is getting married and moving to Buffalo. Stephen doesn't usually drink in the day, but he had two glasses of wine before one o'clock; on an empty stomach, the wine has given him indigestion and a slight headache.

The house is quiet. He stands in the foyer for a moment. He is never home at this time, the middle of the afternoon on a week day. Usually when he comes home, the house is filled with the sounds of his two children and their friends. He calls, 'Nadine?' once, then, not hearing an answer, goes straight to the den and takes off his shoes and suit jacket, and loosens his tie. He takes two pink tablets of Pepto-Bismol out of the tube he keeps in the pocket of his suit jacket, and crunches them between his teeth. He makes a few phone calls, and then puts his feet up on the coffee table and rests his head against the back of the sofa and closes his eyes.

He is awakened by something, maybe a whisper, or a rustling, and feels cool threads of air twining around his ankles. The room is darkening, and the familiar muffled thump of music throbs from upstairs. The back of Stephen's neck is stiff, and he rotates it a few times, rubbing at it. He passes his hand over his eyes, and licks his lips, then walks upstairs, looking at his watch. It is ten after five.

The master bedroom is empty. 'Nadine?' Stephen says, loudly enough for Nadine to hear him if she is in the bathroom. He waits a second, then goes to Kevin's room. The music through the door is low this time. He doesn't knock, but opens the door and sees Kevin lying on his bed. His eyes are closed. There is a strange smell in the room. Stephen's nostrils widen.

'Kevin,' he says, louder than he needs to. Kevin's eyelids fly open, and he sits up, a dazed look on his face.

'Do you know where your mother is?'

'Mom?' Kevin says, then stares at his father, his mouth open.

'Yes. Your mother. Short blonde hair, grey eyes. About this tall.' Stephen puts his hand to the bridge of his nose. 'Remember her?' His voice is filled with a mocking tone.

Kevin lies back, shutting his eyes again. 'Haven't seen her.'

Stephen shakes his head. 'Turn the music down,' he says, although really, the music is not that loud, for once. 'And what is that smell?'

Kevin doesn't answer, so Stephen reaches for the volume knob of the eight-track and turns it sharply to the left. When he is partway down the hall he hears the volume go up again. He starts to turn back, but stops, and goes to Andrea's door. It is open, and Andrea is lying on the floor, riffling the pages of a magazine. The phone is beside her, its cord stretched across the room.

'Where's Mom?' Stephen asks.

Andrea throws the magazine onto the floor and gets up. 'She's around here somewhere,' she says. 'I'm going out right after supper.' Her eyes flicker to the phone. 'So I need to eat now.'

'Well, go downstairs and see what's for supper then,' Stephen says. He goes back to the hall and knocks on Birdie's door, calling, at the same time, 'Birdie. Birdie? I'm looking for Mrs Ladd.'

When there is no answer, he opens the door and puts his head into the room. There is no evidence that anyone has ever set foot in this room, except that the closet door is open, just a sliver. He hears the slam of a door from downstairs, followed by more slams, cupboard and drawer and fridge, and by the force of the slams he knows it is Andrea. He starts to go downstairs, and at the turn in the landing, he sees, through the arched window, that a very light snow has started to fall. 'It will be gone by tomorrow,' he says.

When he gets to the kitchen, he sees that Andrea is sitting at the table, a full bowl of Alpha Bits in front of her. Stephen also sees that a spoon, clean and dry, lies, bowl down, in the middle of the table, far from the cereal bowl, as if it had been flung there, or dropped from above. In her hands Andrea has a piece of paper.

'Why are you eating cereal at supper time, Andrea?' Stephen asks. He looks at the stove, at the uncluttered counters. There is that same stillness in this room that he had felt earlier in the afternoon. Here in the kitchen it's not just the absence of supper, of any telltale smells or sights or sounds, but something else.

'Andrea?' Stephen says. He moves in front of his daughter, so that he can see her face. She looks up at him, and he sees that her mouth, thin and unadorned, is slightly open, the darkness behind her teeth an open wound. He stares at her. 'Andrea?' he finally says, again.

Andrea makes a fluttering move, a tiny fanning, with the paper in her hand. 'There's one for you, too,' she says.

'One what?' Stephen looks at the paper, then his eyes move along the table, past the upside-down spoon, to two other squares of white, almost imperceptible on the white table top.

He goes to the paper squares and picks them up. Envelopes. On one his name, on the other, Kevin's. For some reason the look of his name, written in Nadine's easy looping scrawl, fills him with a calm, certain acknowledgement. It is almost a relief, really, this final acknowledgement. It is like the telephone call you never wait for, but always know will come, some time in the darkest hour of night, while you are in the middle of a deep, good dream, some time while you are carving a turkey, saying a private thank-you for all you have, some time when you think, for a moment, that you are safe. This is when the call comes.

And Stephen knows, without reading the letter, what it says. He puts it on the table and goes to the back door, hurries, in his stocking feet, across the cold brick of the small courtyard, and looks into the garage. Both cars are still there, side by side, as natural as an old couple in their double bed after fifty years of marriage.

Stephen goes back into the house and takes his keys from the ring he hung them on when he came home. He slips his feet into the old loafers sitting neatly by the back door, and slides his arms into the first jacket he feels in the closet, Kevin's red-and-black checked lumberjacket. Then he goes out to the garage, and gets into the car.

He starts driving down Dunvegan Road, not really believing that he will find her, not really knowing what he will do if he sees her, sees Nadine, but driving because it is something he can do.

And so he is shocked when he does come across Nadine, only five blocks from home.

Birdie is with her, her head large and heavy beside Nadine's small fair one. Birdie has one arm around Nadine's thin waist, her thick, dry-looking knuckles clutching the soft dark wool of the smaller woman's navy pea jacket. The older woman's white purse is slung over her wrist, standing out in sharp relief against Nadine's jacket. In her other hand Birdie carries a brown suitcase.

Nadine carries nothing. Her black purse, on its long leather strap, sways from her shoulder, and her hands, gloveless like Birdie's, seems to trail, the fingers hanging open and loose, at her sides.

Birdie and Nadine are walking in the direction of the subway station. As Stephen stops the car at the red light of the intersection, Birdie and Nadine cross in front of him. Stephen watches Nadine's profile as she passes. Her head is up, her chin pulling her ahead. Her eyes stare at the green light she is walking toward. And Stephen sees that as Nadine walks she picks each foot up high, setting it down with a tiny push, as if she is attempting to burrow the toes of her shoes into the hard concrete, dusted with snowflakes, in front of her.

Her feet move with a sense of purpose, with sureness, as if she is barefoot, back on the farm, walking across a ploughed field, or as if she is carrying an egg held up to the sun, trying not to drop it, concentrating on what it is she sees inside.

Give sorrow words; the grief that does not speak
whispers the o'er-fraught heart and bids it break.

– William Shakespeare
Macbeth

Fourth of October

ON THE FOURTH of October, the pain in Melanie's back explodes. It hurts when she stands, hurts more when she sits back on the edge of the bed. Hobbling to the living room, pushing hard on her back with the heels of her hands, she eases herself down onto the couch, and lies on her side, her knees drawn up.

'What are you doing there?' Seamus asks, coming in from the bathroom, rubbing at his hair with a towel. He turns on the television to the weather channel. 'Doesn't your shift start at seven?'

'Yeah. But there's something wrong with my back. I can't go in today.'

Seamus comes over and stands behind the couch, staring at the television. 'Are you sure?'

Melanie closes her eyes. 'Sure about what? About whether I've got a backache? Or that I can't go to work?'

'It's just that it's....' He stops. A big-band version of 'Don't Cry for Me, Argentina' shrills from the television. 'If you don't want to go to work today, stay home. You don't have to pretend there's something wrong with you, Melanie.'

Melanie's eyelids fly open. She slowly turns her head so that she can look up at him. 'Pretend? What's that supposed to mean?'

Seamus's expression doesn't change, his face still directed at the TV. The figures of the temperature and humidity and last year's highs and lows reflect red and yellow on his glasses.

'I thought because of today ... because....'

Melanie struggles to raise herself, grimacing, using her hand along the back of the couch to tug her body into an upright position. A tiny intake of breath, almost a gasp, then a brief whimper of pain slips out from between her sealed lips.

'Say it, Seamus.' At his name the volume grows. 'Say it!'

The loudness of her voice seems to increase the pain.

It had started the day before, just a poke, a nudge, each time she turned a patient or leaned across a bed, but by the time she got home from the hospital it was settling in, a tight, hot band across her lower back.

After supper, sitting on the deck cradling a mug of lukewarm coffee, she started to cross her legs, but the band tightened, stopped her with a sudden sharp stab just above the swell of her right buttock. She took a deep breath and put her feet flat on the deck and looked at the darkening of the leaves on the low, bushy mounds of chrysanthemums that edged the garden.

Melanie used to love the colours of fall; something about the velvety golds, the bronzes and dusty burgundies reminded her of well-aged wines.

'Melanie,' Seamus had called, up to his thighs in coneflowers. Melanie took a sip of her coffee, then leaned forward, carefully, and set the cup on the splintering cedar railing. She looked at Seamus across the small stretch of crisp, browning grass, saw the slight stoop of his back as he carefully studied the blossoms, peering into the bristly black centre of each hoop of orange-gold as if waiting for the flower to tell him something, as if it might whisper 'I'm ready' or 'Go away, not yet.'

'Want some of these for inside?' he asked, not looking up.

Melanie shrugged. 'Sure.'

Seamus had never shown any real interest in the long, narrow perennial garden, until this past spring. In April as soon as the last crusty traces of snow were gone, he'd started to work.

Melanie had watched his activity from the deck. It seemed unnatural, the feverish mulching and weeding, the excitement about overnight growth, each sudden cluster of fresh, luminous green that broke through the soil in its predicted spot.

She, not Seamus, had loved the garden; she had laboured for five springs, adding and separating and cutting back.

'Come see the peonies, Mel,' Seamus had called in May, his

voice almost disappearing as he bent over. 'They didn't even show yesterday.'

Melanie imagined the shiny shoots of the peonies, the tiny nubs of shocking pink, thinking how in other years they had amazed her, the quickness of them stretching up and up, changing colour, so that in less than seven days the stubby domes were gone. In their place were slender green stalks, delicately waving in the breeze she made just walking by.

She remembered showing the starting sprouts to Jeremy, holding his hand, squatting beside him and pointing to the fat shafts of pink, like curious worms poking their sightless heads out of the soil to sniff the spring's warmth. Remembered his fingers, the round baby knuckles and almost transparent nails, reaching out, reaching for the peonies.

She didn't want to see the peonies starting any more, so this year she had stayed on the deck.

* * *

Seamus had kept up his reports all through the summer.

'Looks like this stuff has really spread. All the little mauve and white things. What did you say they were?'

'Artemis,' Melanie said, her voice just loud enough to reach Seamus.

'Yeah. Didn't it just go to the edge of the border last year? Now it's all the way back to here.' He stood still, looking at her, his hands in the pockets of his heavy sweater even though the July sun made long bright pools of heat on the grass and garden.

Melanie looked back at him, but she couldn't see his eyes because of the sun's glare on the lenses of his glasses. She smiled politely.

'Oh, and look,' he'd said, pointing at his right foot, 'you should see how big the....' He stopped, but kept his hand where it was, the long thin index finger still aiming at something on the ground in front of him.

Melanie knew what he was pointing at. She had chosen each spot and put in every plant herself, after all. And as she watched Seamus standing there, pointing, it was as if there were one of those cartoon balloons over his head, filled with the words 'baby's breath'. Melanie felt a sour rush of anger surge up her throat. Anger at Seamus, because she knew he knew what it was, but he couldn't speak the words, couldn't even say 'baby's breath'. But she kept quiet, didn't call out 'What is it? What is it, Seamus, tell me,' forcing him. She let him move on, move away from the bush of tiny white blossoms.

But now, with her curled up in agony on the couch, he has the nerve to question her, question her pain, make her feel there's something wrong with her because her backache coincides with October fourth.

'I KNOW what day it is, Seamus,' she hisses. 'I also know there's something really wrong with my back. Maybe the sciatic; it feels like it's going into my leg.' One hand still clutches the back of the couch, the other runs over the top of her short hair, back and forth. 'And how dare you say I'm pretending? What have I got to pretend about? What? You're the pretender; YOU'RE the one who's always pretending nothing's wrong. That nothing happened.'

Seamus stares down at her, but the colours of the television are still there, on his glasses.

'You just go on, every day, like everything's fine. But it's not.' She licks her lips. 'Our baby died, Seamus, he died, and it's horrible, but you won't even say Jeremy's name, or talk about him.' The words push so hard that her jaw feels like it's dancing on an electrical circuit; she knows that her lips and tongue will be zapped, black and lifeless, if she doesn't get the words out fast enough. 'You pretend nothing's changed. You want to pretend Jeremy never existed, for Christ's sake.' She stares up at him, but it's as if he has no eyes, behind those kaleidoscope lenses. Suddenly she realizes how much it infuriates her, all of it. His glasses, his still body, his quiet acceptance.

'It's not normal, Seamus.' Each shouted word causes a new river of liquid fire down the back of her thigh and into her calf.

'What's wrong with you? Why don't you do something, anything, to show me how you feel? WHAT'S WRONG WITH YOU?'

She realizes her fist is up, over her head, like she's going to punch him somewhere, but he's not close enough, and she uses her clenched fingers to wipe the tears away from her cheeks. 'And don't keep your face like that, like it can't move. I hate it.' She doesn't really hate it, not his face, but she hates the gauze that wraps his features now. The millions of tiny threads that seem to hold everything together have changed his face into the preserved mask of a mummy.

Seamus turns away.

'Don't you go, dammit. Stay here and answer me. Fight with me.' She's shrieking. 'Tell me what YOU'RE going to do today. It's a special day, right? Sort of an anniversary, right, Seamus?' He's standing still, his back to her. 'What are you going to do? How are you going to celebrate Jeremy's death?' She's sobbing, the words coming out in great aching gulps, but she can't stop them. 'I guess I'm celebrating by playing sick, is that what you're saying? So? What are YOU going to do?'

Seamus starts walking. He walks across the living room, to the bedroom, then out again, and Melanie hears the dull thud of the front door.

She loosens her grip on the back of the couch. Her fingers are cramped; she lowers herself and grabs a small vermilion cushion from under her head and presses it against her face, screaming into it. Much later, she lifts the cushion and looks at it, wondering if the stains will ever come out.

* * *

Eventually she phones the hospital to say she won't be in, swallows two small orange capsules from a bottle in the bathroom cabinet, and goes back to bed. She's not tired, but the pills let her drift into a kind of desperate twilight.

Around eleven she rouses herself enough to take two more pills, but no more of the dazed sleep will come. It's after one o'clock when she gingerly moves her legs, gets out of bed and pulls on her plaid flannel housecoat. Then she lets two more of the capsules slide down her throat. She knows she shouldn't; it hasn't been four hours since the last ones, but she needs the numb, faraway feeling they give her.

She shuffles out of the bedroom, stumbling a little as her thick socks catch on the edge of the hall carpet. She goes to the kitchen and runs water into the sink, scooping a handful into her cardboard mouth.

When she turns off the tap, she notices it keeps dripping. She knows it needs a new washer, knows there's a whole jar of washers downstairs in Seamus's room, his basement workshop.

The room is beside the furnace, a cubicle with a long countertop, the walls covered with that board with all the tiny holes in it. In this small, warm, messy room, brightly lit with a buzzing fluorescent tube, Seamus keeps an assortment of tools, dog-eared piles of classic car magazines, an ancient office chair of wood smooth and rich as old honey, and mayonnaise jars and rusting coffee cans filled with nails and screws of all sizes, none of which are ever the right size.

Over this last winter's evenings, while Melanie sat in the living room holding a book in her lap, Seamus was in his workshop. Melanie never heard any sounds coming from it, never saw any evidence of work, like the bookshelves he'd once built for her, or the bird feeder he'd made when Jeremy was six months old. He'd put it up outside Jeremy's window, so from his crib the baby could watch the desperate flutter of the brave sparrows pushing and digging through the soft snow that kept falling on the tray of seeds that whole winter.

A few times she'd asked him about it, what he was doing, all those hours in the workshop.

'Just sorting through things,' he'd say, 'reorganizing,' although when Melanie had gone in there, a few weeks ago, to get a screwdriver to fix the bathroom doorknob, it looked as chaotic as always.

She runs her hands along the collection of river rocks lined up on the windowsill over the sink, feeling the fine silty layer of dust coating them. Then she glances up, out the window, to the backyard.

Seamus is sitting on the top step of the deck.

She makes her way to the back door and opens it, but has to stand still for a moment, her hand on the door jamb, and steady herself, blinking a few times in the cool bright light of the October afternoon. When she calls to Seamus, her voice sounds higher than usual to her own ears; it has a thin, hollow ring, like music played in an empty room.

'What're you doing home?' She leans against the door frame.

'Slow,' Seamus finally says, in his usual voice, as if it had been a usual day. 'Hardly any customers.'

Melanie steps out onto the deck, looks down at the top of Seamus's head, at the thick, red-gold hair. Hair the colour of a maple, after the first frost. Then she sees the box in his lap. He's holding it with both hands. She recognizes it, a rectangular metal cookie tin decorated with a castle, and surrounded by billows of fog, or mist. Scottish shortbread; she got it as a gift once, long ago, from someone at work. She knows she's seen it, the tin, somewhere recently, somewhere that surprised her, where it didn't seem quite right.

Even though Seamus has spoken to her, there's something in the air, some stillness that Melanie can't understand. At first she thinks it's Seamus's anger, like a cloud, like the mist on the tin, swirling and hovering. She lowers herself beside him, one leg stretched out to take the strain off her back, and her knee brushes against his. When he leaves his leg touching hers, she realizes it's not anger, after all.

She doesn't look at him, but at the cookie tin. His thumbs rub slow small circles on the patterned top. She remembers where she saw it.

'Got one of your nail collections in there?' she asks. Stupid question, but she wants to start something, wants him to talk, wants to somehow puncture the dense atmosphere, make a hole in it with her words, so she'll be able to suck some air through, be able to breathe easier.

Seamus makes a sound, not a yes or no, just a faint murmur, and she looks up from the tin. Studying him, the straight line of his nose, she notices he hasn't got his glasses on. He only used to wear them for driving, but some time over the winter, she's not sure when, he started wearing them all the time.

He still doesn't look at her, but his thumbs stop moving. One perfect oak leaf corkscrews gracefully in front of them, landing on the toe of Melanie's sock.

Seamus looks down at the leaf, then takes the lid off the tin, and opens the creased tissue paper.

Melanie sees shoes, the small white shoes with scuffed toes, each shoelace threaded through a little bell.

Seamus picks one shoe up, out of its nest of rustling yellow paper. The bell gives a muted chime, a tiny protest at being moved, as he puts it in his left palm. The shoe reaches from the base of his wrist to the middle of his heart line.

'Remember when we bought these?' he says. 'He was just starting to walk.'

Melanie can't look at him. She keeps her eyes fixed on the shoe, although it's gone all flat and blurry.

'You wanted to get him those little red ones, with straps,' Seamus continues, 'but Jeremy wanted these. He kept reaching for them, and shaking them so the bells rang. Remember?'

Melanie leans her head against his arm.

'And we always knew where he was, by the sound of the bells,' Seamus says, putting the shoe back beside the other, covering them slowly, his hands resting on the tissue paper before he puts the lid on the tin. Then he sets it down on the step, beside him, and looks at her.

Melanie lifts her head off his arm. She can see herself in his pupils, but there's something wrong with his eyes, or maybe it's hers, from all the pills. She sees herself over and over, reflected back, like a room of mirrors. 'I forgot how blue your eyes are,' she says, and wipes her nose with the sleeve of her housecoat.

He turns away, looks at the garden. 'I was thinking of

transplanting some of the peonies this afternoon. Didn't you say that fall is the best time for dividing peonies, for moving them?' He looks back at her, his eyes still that brilliant blue.

Melanie nods. 'I'll come with you,' she says.

'Won't it hurt your back?'

'No,' Melanie says. She brushes a piece of dry brown leaf off the front of Seamus's sweater, stands up and takes a step towards the garden. She feels Seamus move behind her, feels his breath on the back of her neck.

'No,' she repeats. 'It's better if I walk.'

And one trembles to be so understood and, at last,
To understand, as if to know became
The fatality of seeing things too well.

– Wallace Stevens
The Novel, 1950

Willow

WHEN JUDY WAS a much younger woman, she had a friend named Willow. Willow. Such a beautiful, swaying sort of name. Willow was not at that time beautiful or willow-like in any way. She was tall, but big, big everywhere, big and messy. Dowdy, in uniforms of baggy corduroy pants or skirts that brushed her ankles and looked as if they were made from pieces of old bedspreads or curtains. Her breasts swayed loosely, unrestrained under tie-dyed T-shirts or big shirts that might have been worn by a man under a suit at some time. Her dirty-blonde hair was always pulled back into a scraggy ponytail and tied with a piece of thick yarn. She did have fascinating eyes – large and oval, a particular shade of green that was neither olive or hazel, but the sort of green that would bring to mind water – not ocean, not even river, but a quiet lake kind of green, a lake that is warm and shallow, that has a soft bottom, covered with swaying grasses. She never used any make-up. But this was the early seventies, and this type of appearance was not unusual in Judy's neighbourhood; it was probably not unusual in any North American neighbourhood where there were many young children and many young mothers and not much money. Judy was one of the young mothers, too. But unlike Willow, she was small, and she dressed in neatly pressed slacks and flowered, feminine blouses, in cooler weather a creamy cable-knit sweater. Her hair was short and tidy, like the rest of her, in a style they called a pixie cut. Judy wished she had the courage to grow her hair down her back, to wear mismatched clothing. She wished she possessed a name like Willow. But no. It was Judy. Simple and straightforward, as she viewed herself back then.

* * *

Judy met Willow at the little playground not far from her

house. It was late fall, but one of those nice days when summer seems to come back for a few hours. Judy was pushing her older daughter, Amy, in one of the swings. Amy was two and a half. The baby, Caryn, was four months, and asleep in a Snugli on Judy's flat chest. Even though she was still breast-feeding, Judy's breasts had grown smaller, losing tone and shape after the second baby.

Willow didn't appear to be watching any of the children on the swings or slide or climbing apparatus. Instead, she sat on a bench near the sandbox, legs wide apart and her limp skirt drooping in between them as if it held some mysterious object. She had her arms crossed over her own very full chest, and was leaning back against the back of the bench comfortably, her mouth slightly open. She was looking up.

Judy saw her staring at the sky, and glanced upward too, wondering what it was that the woman was looking at. There didn't appear to be anything up there, just blue, scattered with tattered cirrus clouds. Judy continued pushing the swing. Every once in a while she looked back at the woman. The fourth time she looked at her, the big woman lowered her gaze to Judy's and said, 'Do you hear them?'

'Hear what?' Judy asked, mesmerized, for a moment, by the dazzling green of the woman's stare.

'I think it's geese. But I don't see any. And they should have all gone by now. But still, I'm sure I heard them.'

Judy stopped pushing. She put her head to one side and listened. 'No,' she finally said. 'I can't hear anything.'

The woman kept looking into Judy's face. 'Oh, well. Maybe it was something else.' She got up and walked over, peering down at the top of Caryn's head. 'Boy or girl?'

'Another girl,' Judy said, starting to push again. She liked having little girls. She liked dressing them in the matching outfits she made on her old Singer and she especially liked doing all sorts of things with Amy's hair. Caryn didn't have enough yet. And already Amy was good company. Derek was an intern. He was hardly ever home.

The woman reached out and ran her finger over Caryn's

fuzzy dark hair. Judy noticed that the fingernail had something, clay, or maybe putty, around the cuticle.

'You're lucky. I have a boy. He's a great kid, but it's not the same. I always wanted a girl.'

Judy tried to make a sound of sympathy. 'Well, you might still have one.'

The woman took her finger away from the baby's head. 'Nah. One kid's enough.'

'Which one is he?' Judy asked.

The woman looked at her as if she didn't understand the question, then, 'Oh. No, he's not here. He's at school. Grade three.'

Judy nodded. Maybe she's babysitting for someone, she thought. There would be no reason to be at a playground if you didn't have a child with you. 'My name's Judy,' she said. She and Derek had moved, only two weeks ago, from their crowded apartment to the old house the next street over. Judy hadn't met anyone except the neighbours on her left, a quiet older couple who didn't looked pleased as Derek set up the swing set in the patch of grass in the back yard. Judy was looking forward to meeting some of the other women in the area.

'Willow,' the woman said.

Judy looked her. 'Willow? That's your name?' she asked.

The woman nodded.

Imagine. Wait until she told Derek.

* * *

Judy kept running into Willow. Just walking with the girls, or picking up a loaf of bread. They would always stop and chat for a few minutes. Three weeks after their first meeting in the playground Judy saw Willow in the little neighbourhood book store that sold a lot of books on horoscopes and meditation practices. Willow had her son with her. He was a red-haired boy with that pure, milky skin that you know will be trouble later. The boy stood, small and quiet, beside his mother.

'Why don't you come over for coffee?' Willow said.

'All right,' Judy answered, shifting Caryn to her other shoulder. 'When?'

'Right now.'

Judy glanced at her small gold wristwatch. 'Well, it's close to lunch time. Caryn will need a bottle soon.' Judy had given up breast-feeding just before Caryn turned five months. Formula was a nuisance with all the boiling and sterilizing, but Caryn had been sleeping through the night since the first bottle.

'Go home and get one, then come over. She,' Willow had nodded at Amy, 'can have a sandwich with Jason.' She put her hand on Jason's head. 'He's home from school because he has pinkeye.'

Judy instinctively pulled Amy closer against her leg, bending a little and peering into the boy's face. One eye was a little puffed and crusty-looking in the corner. 'Isn't it catching?'

'Not any more. It's pretty well cleared up, but he didn't want to go back yet, so I let him stay home one more day.'

'I think we should make it another time,' Judy said.

'Okay.' Willow took her son's hand. 'I'll call you.'

* * *

She did. A few days after Judy had seen Willow in the book store, the phone rang as Judy was getting the baby out of the bathtub.

'Bring the girls and come over,' Willow said, as soon as Judy had said hello. 'Jason's back at school.'

Judy couldn't think of a reason not to go. She didn't really want to, but didn't know why. 'Okay,' she said. 'Tell me your address.'

'I'm just the street behind you,' Willow said. '127 Morton. The turquoise house with the wind chime.'

As Judy pushed Caryn's stroller down the block, she realized that she'd never told Willow her last name or where she lived.

'How did you get my number?' Judy asked, when they were in Willow's living room. Both girls sat on the little blanket from the stroller. Amy dressed and undressed the doll she'd brought, and Caryn played with a set of big plastic beads that snapped together.

'Oh, everyone knows everyone around here,' Willow answered. 'Nobody moves in or out without people knowing about it. I just asked around.'

'Oh,' Judy said. It hadn't seemed like that kind of neighbourhood to her.

'So what are you doing to the house? I saw a plumbing truck outside the other day.'

'A few renovations. Derek and his brother are going to paint the outside trim this weekend, before it gets too cold. And we're putting a little two-piece bathroom on the main floor. There was a big closet in the front hall, and I'd rather have a bathroom. It's tiring running up and down, especially with toilet training.' She glanced in Amy's direction, raising her eyebrows. 'She's pretty good in the day, but I still put a diaper on her at night. Just in case.'

Willow got up and went over to the little girls. 'What are you doing?' she asked, sitting down cross-legged in front of them. 'A pretty necklace,' she said to Caryn. 'Yes, it's pretty.'

Amy stared at her, then held out her doll.

'Oh, and look at your baby.' Willow took the doll, cuddled it against her chest, then handed it back. 'What a nice baby.' She looked up at Judy. 'Why don't you go and pour us some coffee? It's on the stove. I'll watch them.'

Judy went to the kitchen and hunted around the messy counters and then the crammed cupboard over the stove for clean cups. As she poured coffee into two faded pink melamine mugs, she watched Willow through the doorway. She was unsnapping the beads and handing them, one by one, to Caryn. The baby was smiling, taking each bead and then throwing it down beside her. As Judy watched, Amy shifted over on the blanket, until she was right beside Willow. Willow laughed and put her arm around her.

* * *

A few weeks later, Willow offered to babysit. They were at Willow's kitchen table. She had seen Judy going by and called her in. Judy had been coming back from the library, and was having a hard time pushing the stroller through the slush that covered the sidewalk now. Amy had been whining, holding on to the back of Judy's coat and not wanting to hurry. The wind was making Judy's eyes water and her nose run. She was cold and tired, and Willow said she had just made a fresh pot of coffee.

'It's hard, dragging kids everywhere,' Willow said, once Judy had taken off the girls' jackets and hats and Willow had given each a cracker. 'You should be able to get out by yourself once in a while. The kids will be fine now that they know me. Just give me a couple of days' notice. My hours at the clinic are crazy, but I can pretty well sign in for whatever time I want, as long as I arrange with the other women. So sometimes, when Jason can stay with a friend, I do big long stretches of time, then I'm free for a few days. Lots of times I'm around all day. I could even babysit in the evening, if you and...Darren? no, sorry, Derek, if you and Derek want to go out. I could bring Jason with me.'

'Thanks. Maybe,' Judy said. 'We haven't been out since Caryn was born. Partly because Derek's always at the hospital. Plus the money. We're trying to save everything to put into the house. We still want to get a few more things done before spring.'

Willow's eyes shifted away from Judy, and her lips tightened. Just a tiny bit, but Judy noticed.

'What's wrong?'

'Nothing. Just that...'

'What?'

Willow looked away. 'Oh, people like to talk. You know how they can be. I don't pay any attention.'

'What people? Talk about what?'

'It's not important.'

'Tell me, Willow. What do you mean?'

Willow made an exasperated snort. 'We're not like the rest

of the people around here, Judy. You and I, we mind our own business, get on with our own lives. But some of these women, alone all day, with nothing to think about but what other people are doing, well, they get jealous, gossip. You know.'

'Gossip? About me? Why?'

Again, that shifting of eyes, the uncomfortable shrug. 'I guess because Derek, is, like, you know, a doctor and everything. So you can do all these renovations, fix your house up nicer than the other houses. People are just jealous, that's all.'

'Derek's not a doctor *yet*. He makes peanuts. And all we're doing is some painting, and that new powder room. It's not much.' Judy's voice had risen a half tone, the dropped. 'Actually, Derek's mother gave us the money for fixing up the house. As a house-warming gift. The down payment cleared out our savings, and even with budgeting, it's tight each month.'

'Look, I shouldn't have said anything. Don't even think about it. It's just a few bitchy women, anyway.'

'I met someone named Jessica yesterday. At the Milk Plus a few streets over. She seemed nice. Do you know her?'

'Jessica? Skinny, bad skin?'

Judy thought a moment. 'I guess that could be her. But her skin's not that bad.'

'Yeah. I know her. But she's got problems. I wouldn't get involved with her.'

'Oh,' Judy said. She didn't ask Willow what Jessica's problems were, even though she wanted to know.

'So do you want me to sit for you sometime?' Willow poured Judy more coffee, and pushed the cream container across the table. Judy noticed that Willow had cream now, after she had been over to Judy's and Judy had told her that she and Derek always used cream in their coffee; Derek thought coffee tasted watery with milk. Amy wanted another cracker. Willow got up and found an arrowroot cookie for her, and filled a little plastic Sesame Street cup with apple juice. She picked Caryn up from the floor at Judy's feet. The baby settled against Willow and started to suck the top button of Willow's shirt.

'Sure,' Judy finally answered, watching Caryn. 'Why not?'

* * *

The next week Judy made plans to go shopping for the kids' Christmas presents. Willow said she was expecting an important phone call and didn't want to leave the house, so Judy took the girls over to Willow's and left the three of them dumping out Jason's plastic bucket of Lego in Willow's sunny living room.

'Make sure Caryn doesn't swallow any of the small pieces,' Judy said. 'She's awful for putting things in her mouth.'

'Judy,' Willow said. 'I'm a mother. I know.'

'Sorry. I'm just not that comfortable leaving them anywhere. I wish I had some of my family here. There *is* Derek's mother, and she doesn't mind babysitting every once in a while. But she lives on the other side of the city, and it's awkward packing everything up and –'

'Go,' Willow said. 'Everything will be fine.'

'Go, Mommy,' Amy said.

'Okay.' Judy kissed the girls. Caryn's face started to crumple as Judy said, 'Bye-bye,' but Willow immediately picked her up and showed her a sparkling prism hanging beside the spider plant in the front window. Caryn didn't notice when Judy slipped out the door.

She had been shopping for about an hour and a half when an uneasy feeling hit her. Nothing certain, just a general wave of concern. Fingering the round nose of a musical clown she was thinking of buying for Caryn, she suddenly thought about Willow. How little she knew about her. She'd run into Jessica at Milk Plus and asked her if she knew Willow, but Jessica said she'd never met her. She thought of the way Caryn's face had started to wrinkle with dismay as she was leaving. Of Amy's unconcerned humming as she snapped one Lego piece onto another. Suddenly it was hard to breathe. She dropped the clown back into the bin and ran to the cash register.

'Excuse me,' she said, ignoring the fact that the cashier was ringing in a stout man's purchase. 'Is there a phone I can use?' She was digging through her purse without looking, her fingers passing over her wallet and hairbrush and wads of Kleenex and a soother of Caryn's, feeling for the piece of paper where she'd written Willow's phone number.

The cashier didn't look up from the till. 'Public phones are near the exit.'

Judy saw the black phone on the counter, close to the woman's elbow. She pulled the paper from her purse. 'Couldn't I use that one?'

The woman counted out the man's change and put it in his hand.

'Can I?' Judy asked again, this time reaching toward the phone.

The woman shook out a paper shopping bag with a snap. 'It's not for public use. You'll have to use the phones by the exit.'

'But it's an emergency,' Judy said, with a slight tremor in her voice, the knife edge of panic she was trying to push down. 'Please.'

Frowning, the woman shoved the phone toward her. 'All right. But hurry. I could get in trouble.'

Judy's fingers were shaking as she dialled the numbers. I'm being silly, she said to herself. Just silly. Answer, Willow. Answer. She flexed her calves, going up and down on her toes, just a tiny bit, the way Amy did when she was holding it in and didn't want to use the potty.

The phone rang and rang. Judy saw it ringing, on the wall in Willow's kitchen. She put the heavy black receiver down on the counter, the ringing still audible, and ran down the wide aisle leading away from the counter. Her shopping bag banged against her leg.

'Well, thank YOU,' the cashier said, replacing the receiver with an annoyed clunk. 'Some people.' The stout man nodded in sympathy.

* * *

'I don't know what happened to me,' Judy said, telling Derek about it the next morning, when he got back from the hospital. 'I felt like something awful had happened, that maybe Willow had done something weird, like...I don't know, kidnapped them or something. I must have looked like a madwoman, racing up the steps. Pounding on the door, rattling the knob. Then when I ran into the back yard and saw them there, the kids all bundled up, their cheeks so pink, and Willow pushing them around in an old wheelbarrow, all of them laughing, I didn't know what to say. She knew something was wrong. I made some excuse about feeling sick.'

'Didn't you say she has her own kid?' Derek was spreading marmalade on a piece of toast.

'Yeah. A boy. And I don't REALLY think she would have done anything, but suddenly I got this awful feeling, and I guess I panicked.'

'I thought you liked her.'

'I do. At least I think I do. She's always nice, and Amy and Caryn have really taken to her. Jason – that's her son – he's okay, too, ordinary. It's not like there's anything...' Judy searched for the word, 'suspicious about her. There's just something ... I can't put my finger on it. There's something about her that's different. But I don't know what.'

'Where's her husband?'

'She never said. Just that she was alone. I asked if she was divorced, and she said no. So then I thought maybe he died, and I didn't want to start prying. She talks so much about everything else, but she never mentions Jason's dad.' She picked a crust from Derek's plate, and chewed on the end. 'You've met her. What do you think of her?'

Derek swallowed loudly, then yawned. 'I don't know. We never really had anything to say to each other.' Derek and Willow had crossed paths when Derek would arrive home from the hospital and Willow was sitting in the kitchen with Judy. She always left almost as soon as he came in. 'She seems friendly enough. Probably just lonely. I'm going upstairs to bed for a few hours. Don't let me sleep too long.'

'I won't,' Judy said. 'You don't have another shift tonight, do you?'

'Yeah. It's been murder.'

'I wish you didn't have to be away at night so much. I don't like being alone with the kids.'

Derek kissed her forehead. 'Sorry, Jude. I know.'

* * *

'Are you feeling better?' Willow asked, later that afternoon. She was on her way to pick up Jason from school, and had dropped by Judy's first.

'Oh yeah, I'm fine. It must have been some kind of twenty-four-hour thing,' Judy answered, on her hands and knees on the kitchen floor, throwing toys into a plastic tub. She kept her head down.

'Probably Derek brings home germs from the hospital,' Willow said, stooping to pick up a stuffed puppy. She stroked its synthetic fur.

'Maybe.' Judy sat back on her heels. 'I can't keep this place tidy. The only time I can pick up a bit is when the girls are napping. But as soon as they wake up, it starts all over.'

'He works a lot, doesn't he?' Willow asked.

'Well, he's interning. They get stuck with all the worst shifts, and work the longest hours. It's all part of the package.'

'Does he always work at night?'

'No. But a lot of the time.'

'Oh,' Willow said. Not just oh, but oooh.

Judy threw her a quick look, but Willow was looking out the window at the swing set.

'How long have you two been married?'

'Four years,' Judy said, still looking at Willow. Willow suddenly turned toward Judy, and there was something on her face that Judy couldn't name.

'I saw him a few nights ago,' Willow said. 'I guess he was coming home. It was around midnight.'

Judy thought for a minute. 'Which night?'

Willow shrugged. 'It was Friday. Jason had a sleepover at his friend's, and I had worked the four-to-midnight phone line. I was on my way home when I saw him.'

Judy went to the back door and checked the big calendar tacked onto the painted wood.

'I honked at him, but I guess he didn't recognize me.'

'Well,' Judy said, her finger on the calendar, 'I'll have to ask him about it. He was in Emergency all night. Friday? Are you sure?'

'Mmm-hmm,' Willow said. She brushed the fur away from the puppy's face and studied the hard brown plastic eyes, then glanced at the clock on Judy's stove. 'Don't bother him about it. It doesn't matter. I have to run. Jason will be out in a few minutes. I'll call you tomorrow.'

'Okay,' Judy said. She studied the calendar for a few minutes, and then Amy wandered into the kitchen, rubbing her eyes and wanting a glass of juice.

* * *

'It wasn't me,' Derek said, when Judy told him about Willow. 'I was at the hospital until seven Saturday morning.'

'She said it was. She even honked.'

'Well, she's wrong.' Caryn was crawling across the carpet in front of him. 'C'mere, you little pudge,' he said, getting down on the floor beside her. He pulled up her shirt and blew on her stomach, making gulping noises and nibbling at her. Caryn screeched with delight, and Amy ran over and jumped on Derek's back.

Judy watched them playing, biting a piece of loose skin on the edge of her thumb.

* * *

The next day it was cold, with the wind throwing hard, bitter chips of snow against the windows. After Derek went to the hospital Judy locked the doors and went upstairs to the girls' bedroom and played with them there. She brought their lunch upstairs and they had a picnic on the floor, then she put them down for their naps and went to her own room and lay down with a book and tried to read. The phone rang beside her. Judy looked at it, then reached down and unplugged it. It kept ringing in the downstairs hall, every half an hour until after four o'clock. Each time it rang over fifteen rings. Judy counted the rings, but she didn't answer it. Derek never phoned her from the hospital.

The snow kept up all night, but had stopped by morning, and the sun, weak but persistent, was making the small drifts on the steps shimmer. Willow was at Judy's back door before the girls had even finished their breakfast. She was carrying a big Tupperware container.

'Look what I've got,' she said, peeling back the lid. There were at least two dozen buns, fragrant and heavy with raisins. 'Cinnamon buns. I made them yesterday. It was such a gloomy day and there was nothing else to do. These are for you.'

Judy took the container. 'Thanks, Willow. But don't give me the whole container. We'll never eat them all. I'll just take a couple out. You take the rest home.'

Willow pressed the container against Judy's midriff. 'No. I want you to have them. Freeze some.' The two women were still in the doorway. 'Did you have a busy day yesterday?'

Judy's cheeks were warm. 'Yeah,' she lied. 'I had some errands to do.'

'Poor you.' Willow's voice was sympathetic. 'It was an awful day for going out. I hope Derek left you the car.'

'Yeah,' Judy said again. She fingered the edge of the Tupperware.

Willow craned her neck to see around Judy's head, into the kitchen. 'Do you like cinnamon buns, Mamie Amy?'

Amy looked up from her Cheerios. She nodded, pushing away her bowl. Milk slopped onto the table. 'I have a bun, Mommy?'

'I guess so.' Judy let a few seconds of silence pass. Willow was standing, politely, in front of her. 'Come on in,' Judy finally said. 'The kitchen's getting cold with the door open.'

* * *

'She sounds like she's lonely.' Joy drained the last drop of white wine from her glass. Joy was Judy's older sister. The worst of the winter was over, and some mornings almost felt spring-like. Joy had flown in to stay with Judy for a week, a little visit. Sitting in the living room, late at night on the first day Joy had arrived, Judy had been describing Willow to her, telling her how she was always doing her favours, always dropping over, bringing little treats for the girls, phoning late at night when she knew Derek was at the hospital, to see if Judy was all right.

'That's what Derek says. It's just that she's so ... well, nice to me,' Judy said. 'And I appreciate it, I do. She's really smart, and we talk about all kinds of things. She used to be a social worker, some position where she had a lot of authority, but then she got fed up with it all, said she was sick of being treated like she didn't know anything, and quit. Now she works at the crisis centre, counselling. She says it's not good pay, but she can get by. She works weird hours, and she seems to be home a lot. So when she comes over, even though in one way I don't want her here, in another way I do. It gets lonely, with just the kids, and Derek away so much of the time.'

'Why don't you do something? Take a course, maybe finish your degree. You can get a sitter in a few times a week.' Joy was eight years older than Judy. She had married young and had three children in three years. They were all teenagers now, and Joy had started her own catering business. 'I remember what it's like, being shut in with kids all day. You go a little crazy. Get her, that Willow friend of yours to babysit. Sounds like a perfect situation.'

'I know she would. But I don't think I want her to.' Judy thought for a moment. 'It's like she's jealous or something. Like she doesn't want me to have any other friends. She always wants to know what I'm doing, where I'm going. I'm starting to hide from her. Hide, Joy, in my own house. She always seems to be at the door, or phoning about something.'

Joy chopped her hand through the air as if she were cutting

something off in front of her face. 'So tell her to lay off.' Joy had always been bold, outspoken. Judy admired her. Joy had never been afraid of their parents the way Judy was. She had stuck up for Judy when they were kids. Judy felt safe when Joy was around.

'That's easy for you to say, Joy. Wait until you meet her, then you'll see what I mean. I bet she'll be around tomorrow. Even though I told her I'd be busy all week, because you'd be here, she'll find some excuse. Maybe Caryn left one of her toys there, or she found a recipe for some kind of cookies she knows Amy would love. She uses anything as an excuse.'

'Right,' Joy said. She poured herself another glass of wine and raised it in a mock toast. 'To Willow. I can't wait.'

* * *

Judy couldn't believe what Joy had to say about Willow.

'A lesbian? Joy! How can you say such a thing?'

Joy minced onion for the spaghetti sauce. 'Wake up, Judy. She's a dyke, for sure.'

Judy let out a brief moan and slumped against the counter. 'Don't say that. It makes me sick.'

'Why? You should be flattered. She couldn't take her eyes off you.'

'That's not true!' Judy stirred the browning ground beef, hitting the wooden spoon against the sides of the big pot with a dull knocking. She stopped in the middle of one of the swishing circles. 'Ha! She can't be. She has a child.'

Joy closed her eyes for a second. 'What? Lesbians can't have sex with a man? Can't get knocked up? God, Judy, you're more naïve than Wendy.' Wendy was Joy's youngest child. She was thirteen.

Judy stirred more gently now. 'But I would know, wouldn't I, Joy? I would know if she was attracted to me like – like *that*. Wouldn't I?' She looked at her sister.

Joy grinned. 'You'll never change, Judy. But you shouldn't let her take over if it's bugging you. Just tell her you need some space. Head space. Willow looks like the kind of person who knows about head space.' She scooped up the onion. 'You ready for this?'

* * *

Judy really didn't believe Joy. Joy had always been melodramatic, an alarmist. But she couldn't get the idea out of her head. 'Damn you, Joy,' Judy said, or thought, many times after Joy had left. She started watching Willow more carefully, looking for hidden meanings in the things she said. It was hard to know what to look for, but Judy definitely felt uncomfortable. She couldn't talk easily with Willow any more. Once, when they both reached for the sugar spoon at the same time, and Willow's fingers brushed hers, Judy snatched her hand away, then felt foolish, and started babbling about a new sugar substitute she'd read about.

'Are you okay?' Willow asked, when Judy finally stopped the meaningless chatter.

'What do you mean?' Judy got up, too quickly, and grabbed Caryn and checked her diaper. Caryn squawked and struggled to get down and go back to her Fisher Price Stack-A-Set.

'You seem jumpy.' Willow came over to Judy and looked into her face. Willow's eyes were moist, concerned. 'Is it you and Derek? Problems?'

'No.' Judy's voice was sharp. 'No. There's nothing wrong with Derek and me. Nothing. In fact,' Judy turned her back on the kids, facing Willow, 'we've even been trying for another baby.'

Willow's expression changed. 'Really.' She stepped away from Judy, back to the table, and picked up her coffee. 'Aren't you the brave one.'

It wasn't true at all. Judy didn't know why she said it. She and Derek had once talked about having three kids, maybe even four. But that had been a long time ago, before Caryn was born. Lately, things really hadn't been that great between them. Not with Derek working all hours, and Judy always worn out because of the constant demands of a baby and a toddler. Judy could hardly remember when they'd last had a good conversation. Or laughed about anything. Or had sex. It seemed that if one of them wanted it, the other was too tired.

* * *

When the weather turned balmy, Derek's mother invited Judy and the girls up to her cottage. The water was still too cold for swimming, but the kids could play in the sand. It would be a nice break, Derek told her, go, relax, let Mom help with the kids.

'Okay,' Judy said, although she wasn't sure she'd be able to relax, alone with Derek's mother for a whole week.

'I'll get a few days off and drive up,' Derek promised. 'Mom can watch the kids and maybe we can even sneak off to Briarcrest Lodge for a night.' They'd spent their honeymoon at Briarcrest.

Judy put her arms around Derek's neck. 'That would be great. It's been so long since we've had any time alone.'

'Are you sure your friend Willow will manage without you? Won't be too jealous, you going off and leaving her behind?'

Judy dropped her arms. 'What do you mean?' She hadn't told him what Joy had said. It was too embarrassing.

'Just joking,' Derek said. He winked at her. 'Remember the hot tub? Bring that bathing suit you wore on our honeymoon.'

'As if it would still fit,' Judy said.

* * *

The day before she left, Judy told Willow she was going away for a week, to Derek's mother's cabin. She told Willow there was no phone, even though there was. She didn't tell her the exact location, just that it was west. Willow said nothing.

Judy ended up staying an extra week. Derek's mother hadn't been as critical of the children as she had been in the past, or Judy's disciplining of them, and seemed to enjoy talking with Amy now, colouring and helping her put puzzles together. She even helped with the dressing and feeding of Caryn. Derek did take two days off, and surprised Judy by having a bottle of champagne and a fruit basket waiting in the room for them at Briarcrest. That first night, Judy and Derek sat on their balcony and drank all the champagne and then went down to the hot tub near the pool. After a few minutes in the steamy, swirling water, Judy started giggling, and they hurried back to their room and made love on a towel Derek put down on the balcony. Judy liked opening and closing her eyes as she lay on her back, seeing the stars pulse and waver above Derek's head. The only thing that spoiled the mood for Judy was that in one swift flash, just a split second, really, Willow's face appeared among the stars.

* * *

Judy came back feeling rested and calm; she had a bit of a tan and she'd made the decision to let her hair grow. Maybe even put some lighter streaks in it. She'd never had long hair.

She didn't call Willow. And surprisingly, Willow didn't call her. Judy continued to feel relaxed.

Five days passed. It was a beautiful June day, and Judy was on her way back from enrolling Amy for the fall session of the nursery school in the St. Eustace Anglican church basement. She decided to stop at the library and let the kids get out some books. When they were done and she was humping the stroller down the three broad steps, the back of the stroller loaded with books and Amy carrying her purse for her, she saw Willow standing on the pavement in front of the library.

Something was wrong with Willow. She'd lost weight, a lot of weight, in the less than three weeks since Judy had seen her. Her face was older, haggard, and although she'd always been messy, now she looked as though she'd been sleeping in her clothes.

They stared at each other.

'You're back,' Willow finally said.

'Willow. What's happened?'

Willow stood still, staring into Judy's face, then her own face did something odd, something Judy had never seen before, a strange working, then collapsing.

There was nothing for Judy to do but to put out her arms,

and Willow came into them. As she wrapped her arms around Willow's hard back, she noticed how warm Willow was. Hot really, unnaturally hot, as if she had a fever. And Judy could smell something, an odour, rising up from the open neck of Willow's shirt. It was a deep, earthy smell, but not unclean. No, it was somehow a green smell, reminding Judy of spring.

* * *

It had been the most awful experience she'd ever had, Willow told Judy later, after Caryn had been put down and Amy was in front of the television. He was all right now, the tumour was benign, but, Oh Judy, Willow had said, starting to weep again, to see your own child lying there, see him wheeled into the operating room and knowing he might not be alive the next time you saw him.

'And there weren't any obvious signs?' Judy asked, her mind racing over her own children's recent health.

'Nothing. Just a stomach ache, off and on, for a few days. No fever or anything that seemed really serious. But on the third day, I knew he was in more pain than a normal stomach ache, and took him to the doctor. He asked all the usual questions about diet, bowel movements, anything new in his routine, but there was nothing. He was going to send him home, telling me it might be an allergy to milk, to take him off all dairy products and see what happens, but I said no, I told him I wanted Jason to have some tests. If I hadn't insisted, Jude, hadn't MADE that doctor schedule tests right away....' Willow shook her head, passing her hand over her eyes, and Judy put her own hand on Willow's wrist, squeezing it gently.

'It's a really weird kind of tumour, one they hardly ever see in kids, the doctor told me later,' Willow eventually went on. 'And while it wasn't cancerous, it would have eventually caused some obstruction that might have been fatal.' She looked down at Judy's hand on her wrist. 'I felt so alone, Judy. I've never felt so alone in my whole life, sitting in that hospital.'

'Were you at the Mount D? Where Derek works?'

Willow shook her head. 'No. I tried and tried to get in touch with Jason's dad, for some support, but he was never home.'

So he is alive, Judy thought, then was immediately guilty that she was more concerned with finding out this detail than thinking about Jason.

'I have to get going,' Willow said. 'He's coming out of the hospital tomorrow morning. I just came home to get in a few groceries.' Again she looked down at Judy's hand still cradling her wrist.

Judy couldn't think of anything to say. 'Well, I'm back, Willow,' she said, when the silence stretched. She could feel Willow's blood thumping in her palm. And again, the hot, dry feel of her. 'I'm here now.'

* * *

Derek didn't know what kind of tumour it could have been. 'Ask her the name of it,' he said. 'There's probably a name for whatever it was he had. It doesn't sound like anything I've heard of. Who's her doctor?'

'I don't know,' Judy said, hardly able to keep the irritation out of her voice. She wasn't sure why she felt annoyed with Derek's questions.

'No,' Derek said, picking a slice of peach out his pie with his fork. 'I've never heard of anything like that, an abdominal tumour, with no other symptoms but a stomach ache.'

'So what are you saying?' Judy got up from the kitchen table and started running water into the sink. 'Are you saying she's lying?' She turned off the faucet and turned to face Derek. 'Is that what you're saying?'

Derek ate his last bite of pie. 'I wasn't even thinking that, Judy. I just thought she must have forgotten to tell you something. Why? Do *you* think she's lying?'

'Of course not!' Judy watched the water go down the drain. 'You should have seen her. Nobody could look like that unless they had been through an awful time. She was really a mess. And she seemed so, well, so sad. And smaller, somehow.'

'Smaller?'

'Yeah. She's lost weight.'

'She phoned when you were the cottage, after the first week, looking for you.'

'What did you tell her?'

'That you weren't coming back right away. That you were taking an indefinite holiday.'

'Why did you say that? You knew when I was coming home.'

Derek shrugged. 'I don't know. It just got to me, her phoning first thing in the morning and waking me up after an eighteen-hour shift. I was pissed with her, and told her not to call here, that you'd probably call her when you got home. But every time I was home there was at least one hang-up. I figured it was her, checking.' He drained his glass of milk. 'Anyway, whatever I feel about her, I hope her kid's all right.'

'Me too,' Judy said. 'I hope he's all right.'

* * *

'I came as soon as I could,' Judy said. She set Caryn down. The baby started to whine, and Judy rattled her keys and then gave them to her. Caryn stopped fussing and jingled the keys in one chubby fist.

'Where's Amy?'

'She's playing at a friend's house.'

'Whose?'

Judy took a Kleenex out of the pocket of her shorts and wiped Caryn's nose. 'Just someone on our street. You don't know them.'

'Maybe I do. What's their name?'

Judy straightened up. 'Willow. You said I had to come right away. Caryn was still sleeping, and I got her up. I thought something must be wrong. Is it Jason? Is something wrong?'

'No. He's doing great. You know kids; they bounce back so fast. I just made some strawberry jam, and I wanted you to try it. I got some fresh bread from the bakery, and I thought we could have a tasting party.'

'What?' Judy said. She looked around the living room. 'Where's Jason?'

'Oh.' Willow gave a little laugh. 'His dad finally got in touch with me, actually right after I got back from your house the other day. He wanted to take Jason to his place to recuperate, so I let him.'

'You let him?'

'Yeah. Ed, that's Jason's dad, he's laid off right now, and can be with Jason all the time. It's easier for me, and better for Jason. I couldn't leave him with his usual babysitter when I go to work – she's got about six kids at her place all the time, and Jason has to be closely watched, the doctor said, not move around too much until the incision heals. Why? Do you think I shouldn't have let him go with Ed?'

'No. No, it's none of my business. It's just that you've never even mentioned Ed before. I didn't think Jason had any contact with his father. And now he's staying with him.'

Willow shrugged. 'We keep in touch. And I learned a long time ago you have to go with the flow, Judy. Do what's best for everyone.'

'I guess so,' Judy said. 'Look, Willow, you shouldn't have called me like that, told me you needed me to come over right away. Been so secretive. It's not right. Like I said, Caryn was asleep and Amy is with her friend. I was in the middle of filling out some forms. The house was quiet, for once. I don't get much quiet time. And then you called, and I dropped everything and came running over here, because I thought you were in some kind of trouble. That there was a problem with Jason.'

'Forms for what?'

Judy didn't answer for a few seconds. 'For university. I decided to go back, part-time. Finish my degree.'

'Oh. Well, do you want to try that jam?'

'I don't think so. I'm going to go back home. I have a lot to do before supper.'

'You're not staying?'

'I said no, Willow.'

Willow sat down on the couch. 'But I don't really feel that

well. I'm still really upset about Jason, Judy. I need you to stay for a while.'

'You look much better already,' Judy was looking down at Willow.

'Do you think so? I feel better, now that you're back, and I have someone to talk to, to share things with again.' She took Judy's hand in both of hers.

Judy looked down at their joined hands. 'And because Jason's going to be fine.'

'Well, of course. Of course.'

'What was the name of his tumour?'

'Name?' Willow asked, letting go of Judy's hand and standing so they were face to face, only inches apart. 'They don't give names to tumours.'

'Sometimes they do, Derek told me. Or at least, they name the problem, if it's a syndrome or something.'

Willow looked behind Judy. 'Caryn's about to chew on that plant. Caryn, sweetie, don't eat that. It can make you sick.'

Judy half turned toward Caryn. 'So you didn't ask what Jason's problem was called? Or you just don't remember any name the doctor gave you?'

'No.' Willow's voice was lower, but louder. 'I *did* ask, and I *did* write it down. It's somewhere in all this junk. I'll dig it up. For Derek.' The k had a particularly hard sound.

'Okay,' Judy said, and took the baby away from the dusty philodendron in a corner of the living room.

'Bye-bye,' Caryn said, over Judy's shoulder.

* * *

'Judy?'

Judy sat straight up in the dark, suddenly wide awake, surprised and yet not surprised to hear Willow's voice on the phone.

'Jude?'

'What is it?'

'Are you in bed?'

'Of course.' Judy glanced at the illuminated dial of the clock on the bedside table. 'It's after one. I was sound asleep. What are you calling about?'

Silence, then,'Derek's on nights, right?'

'Yes.' She turned on the lamp beside the clock. 'What do you want, Willow?'

There was a muffled sound. 'I'm scared, Judy.'

'What's wrong?'

'I'm not sure. I heard something, and I went downstairs.' There was the sound of something – a hand, or a piece of cloth – covering the receiver. Then that same muffled noise.

Judy pushed back the covers and swung her legs over the side of the bed. 'Are you all right? Is someone there? Willow? Willow, answer me.'

The receiver cleared again. Judy heard Willow hiccup. 'I'm not sure, Judy. I keep hearing things, and ... and I'm scared.'

'Did you call the police?'

'No.'

'Why not?'

'Would you come over?'

Judy sighed. 'Of course I can't, Willow. I can't leave the children. Look, hang up and call the police. Tell them you hear something, a prowler. They'll come and check.'

'Can I come there, then?'

Judy closed her eyes, putting her head back so that when she opened her eyes she saw the ceiling. The ceiling had been spackled by the previous owners, probably covering cracks in the plaster, Derek had said. The spackle was the kind with those tiny glittery flecks. Some of them caught the glare of the lamp. Judy thought of the night sky over the balcony at Briarcrest Lodge, and had to close her eyes again. 'Willow?' There was a breath of a sigh in the way she said the name.

'Yes?'

'Don't call me any more, okay?'

'What?' Willow said, in that same disbelieving way Judy had said the word earlier that day, when she realized why Willow had asked her to come over. 'What?' Willow repeated.

'Don't call, Willow. You can't phone me from now on. Or come over.'

In the long hush that followed her words, and in the darkness behind her tightly closed lids, Judy thought she heard the sounds of Amy and Caryn, in their room next door, breathing.

Finally, 'What did I do, Judy? Tell me. What?'

Judy let her eyelids release so just a slit of light came in. The room lost its focus; Derek's jeans, lying over the chair under the window, grew larger, their edges woolly. 'I need space, Willow. I'm going back to university in the fall. Amy will be in nursery school, and I'm taking both girls to a sitter when I'm at classes.

'What sitter, Judy? I could arrange my work hours. I could babysit for you. I wouldn't even charge.'

Judy forced the air through her lips. 'Stop it, Willow. I've got it all arranged.'

'Please, Jude.' It was a whisper.

'No,' Judy whispered back. 'No.' Then she set the receiver into its cradle so gently that it didn't make a sound.

* * *

Almost two decades later Judy is at the ballet. It's November, and the ballet is Tudor's *The Leaves Are Fading*. Judy can only afford to go to the ballet once or twice a year, and this year she was determined it wouldn't be December, and *Nutcracker*. With all three of her daughters interested in dancing, over the years she has seen *Nutcracker* more times than she cares to think about.

This time it is only Tamara, her youngest, with her. The two older girls have moved out. Amy is a landscape architect, just getting established, and Caryn is finishing her degree in commerce. Tamara, who came along as a surprise when the marriage was already dead, kept Judy going many times. When Judy used to think back on it she recognized that things started going seriously downhill when they moved from the neighbourhood; they'd left the tall old house right after Judy started at the university. She said she wanted to move so that she could be closer to school and Derek closer to the hospital. And she had decided she wanted a bungalow, she had told Derek; the dark narrow stairs were too hard on her, lugging kids and toys and laundry up and down all day.

Then the baby came along, and she thought it might help, but no, she and Derek parted when Tamara was only eight months old. It had been rough for quite a few years. But Derek was and is a support to his daughters, financially and emotionally, even though he remarried and has two sons. He has a successful general practice in a group downtown.

With many starts and stops, Judy finally finished her Bachelor of Education, and got a job teaching drama and English at the high school level. She likes it. She has a number of friends, and Amy and Caryn drop over more often than she thought they would. Most of the time she believes herself to be content. She has begun thinking that she might start calling herself Judith. She feels it undignified, somehow, a middle-aged woman being called Judy.

At the intermission, standing with their drinks, a white wine spritzer for Judy and a ginger ale for Tamara, Tamara nudges Judy.

'There's a woman over there, staring at you, Mom.'

'Where?' Judy asks, turning.

'Don't look!' Tamara says through clenched teeth, raising her eyebrows in the despairing way of any sixteen-year-old.

Judy obediently lowers her eyes.

'She's in a green dress. Blonde. Tall and thin, and pretty, sort of like Diane Sawyer, or Martha Stewart.'

Judy takes a sip from her plastic glass, her eyes travelling the crowd. When she sees Willow, she forgets to breathe. Judy might not have recognized her if she'd walked past her, that's how different she looks, but staring at her from the distance is a different thing. Judy sees that she is, as Tamara has said, pretty. To Judy, Willow is more than pretty, quite lovely, really. Elegant is the word Judy would use, should anyone ask her. Nothing of the old Willow, except for the facial features. Judy remembers the colour of Willow's eyes, even though she could never think of the right descriptive word for them so many years ago, and knows that Willow has chosen that green dress to emphasize them. And it occurs to Judy that while she has been growing out of her name, Willow has grown into hers.

Judy sees that Willow says something to someone beside her, but the crowd is thick and since Judy is short, she can't get a look at who Willow is talking to. Then Willow looks in her direction again, and for a second her eyes meet Judy's, and Judy sees no look of surprise there, as if Willow has been watching Judy long before Judy saw her. A small smile plays about Willow's full lips, which are a soft apricot colour.

'Do you know her, Mom?' Tamara asks, turning so that she blocks Judy's view of Willow.

'I don't think so,' Judy says, not sure at all why she is lying to her daughter. She has thought about running into Willow so many times over the years that when it finally happens she isn't sure what she wants to do. She doesn't know whether she wants to ignore her, or whether she would like to put her arms around her, feel the length of her body against her own, like she did on the library steps. But at that moment there is the small musical trill that indicates that the intermission is over and the audience is expected back in their seats; the crowd buckles and diffuses in one huge, smooth swell, and Judy loses sight of Willow.

Through the rest of the ballet, Judy scans the audience. There are so many smooth blonde heads in front of her, but Judy knows that none of them are Willow. She doesn't want to turn her head and look to the sides or behind. Or actually, she does want to, but knows it would be inappropriate in the middle of the ballet.

When the final applause fades away, Judy stands quickly, looking in all directions. But although she thinks she catches sight of a tall blonde woman in a green dress slipping out one of the exits, she can't be sure it is Willow. And she almost loses Tamara in the throng as she hurries, practically running, through the milling bodies on their way to the coat check, hoping for one more glimpse, or a scent, of green.

The face is the mirror of the mind, and eyes without speaking confess the secrets of the heart.

– Saint Jerome, Letter 54

Eva's Mirror

'DEAR BELLA,' he started each letter, through the fall and winter and spring and summer, 'All goes well with Eva.'

Then he wouldn't mention Eva again, but instead write about the season, and the kind of weather it offered up this particular year. He might write about the approach of a Canadian holiday and its meaning, or some small fact about Canada that he thought could be informative and interesting for Bella, for her family, perhaps her whole village. Once he wrote about the strange wonder of the flea market at Aberfoyle, once about a pod of whales spotted from a small boat in the Straits of Juan de Fuca, once a description of the lobster traps used in Peggy's Cove. Whatever the topic, Gordon made sure that he wrote in large, legible letters, mindful that the words would have to be translated into Spanish.

He had taken over the letter-writing to Bella when he was going through the files to pay bills, trying to figure out the order Eva had always used. He'd come across the plain manila folder and, opening it, looked at the black-and-white snapshots of the composed little face, growing older with each successive photo, but somehow never losing the slight reproach he felt in her dark eyes.

When he first found the folder from World Vision, he tried to think how long it had been since Eva had written to Bella. He was ashamed to admit, even to himself, that he had all but forgotten about the little girl. The monthly payments were automatically deducted from his bank balance, and he paid little attention to it.

He began to search through the file, looking for the most recent letter from Bella, to see if it gave some indication as to when Eva had last written. As he stooped over the desk in the den, shuffling through the papers in the drawer, he realized, with a heavy draining feeling somewhere in his abdomen, that he was doing exactly what Eva had started doing, at the beginning.

It was this unexplained searching, the endless looking for things, that he noticed when it first started. And perhaps it was this, in the end, that he found hardest to bear witness to. Eva, who always wanted so badly to please, to appease, to find the pen caught amongst the pile of bills on the desk, the television remote down the side of the couch cushion, the grocery list stuck in a magazine. At some point, and Gordon couldn't exactly pinpoint the month, it had become Eva who could not find a thing, spending hours fussing in drawers and boxes and cupboards.

She couldn't seem to go by a mirror or window without stopping and looking. She would touch her face, tentatively, gently, especially around the eyes, the mouth, the small soft pouches of flesh under her jaw. It was as if she were surreptitiously checking for something that might, without her knowing, have been slowly shifting. Something showing itself when it should be hidden, like the lacy hem of a favourite slip, the elastic at the waist suddenly, after the last washing, turning brittle and unreliable.

Gordon watched her, from his chair in the living room, as she spent much time leaning toward the mirror in the hall. The mirror was very old, and made of Venetian glass. They had bought it at an antique store in Quebec City, and brought it home, wrapped in rags the dealer had kindly supplied, in the trunk of their Pontiac Seville. Because of the mirror's age, the surface of the glass was sprinkled with amoeba-like blotches, some dark, some lighter, all marring the glass with shadowy grey shapes. There were plans to have the mirror re-backed; Gordon had even gone so far as to find a place that specialized in the silvering of mirrors, but then everything had started, and he had left it as it was.

Gordon remembered how Eva would lean close to the mirror, her lips falling open, and peer at her reflection. Gordon wondered, after a time, if she even realized that it was not her face so marked, but the mirror, showing its age, hiding secrets.

Was this what had so attracted Eva to the mirror in that dim, dusty shop on the rue St. Paul? She had looked at it again and again, going back to it while Gordon was trying to interest her in a pressed celery dish in the Canadian Thistle pattern, or a tiny millefiori paperweight, resembling a bouquet of massed flower heads captured in glass.

He knew it would be difficult to get the mirror home, all the way through Quebec, Ontario, Manitoba, Saskatchewan, and into Alberta. They couldn't take the chance of having it shipped, and he started calculating, even before Eva turned to him, with that joy in her eyes that he could never dampen by saying no, whether they could fit it into their trunk. They would have to move their suitcases and other small purchases onto the back seat and floor.

'Just look, Gordon,' Eva said, shaking the sleeve of his shirt ever so slightly. 'Look at the way the mirror seems to reflect beyond our own images. It is as if you can see all the beautiful ladies of the past, the ladies who must have stood before this mirror, in Rome, or Florence, perhaps even in Murano itself, where all the mirrors were made. Primping for a dance, for a tea, for the arrival of a special someone. Can you not see it?'

This was the way Eva spoke. She never used contractions, and her English was very correct. Eva had told Gordon – actually, it was on the very night that he proposed to her – that she had worked long and hard on learning proper pronunciations. And so there was no trace of the Hungary of her youth, not an accent, none at all. But there was something in the speech pattern Eva created that set her apart. Whenever they met new people, Gordon thought he detected them turning their heads, very slightly, when Eva spoke, and sometimes, even the slightest wrinkle of concern would flit over their faces, as if listening required a tiny bit more effort than was usual.

Gordon agreed with Eva about the mirror, about its beauty, and about the imagining of the faces. Personally, he found the mirror a bit too ornate, almost, he said to himself, but only once, as he watched the salesclerk write out the receipt, almost bordering on garish. But Eva had seemed so intent, so thrilled, running her fingertips over the glass, then standing back, with arms crossed and eyelids lowered, a small smile turning up the corners of her mouth.

It would be their big purchase for the trip. This was the highlight of each vacation, the discovery and bringing home of a meaningful addition to their home. Their home was tidy and dustless, and filled with beautiful, silent objects.

* * *

It was just after they bought the mirror that Gordon began to wonder about Eva.

He had no reason to suspect anything; she wasn't old, after all, only in her early fifties. Gordon, well into his own middle age, thought this was the most wonderful time for the face of a woman. Although the bloom of any youthful beauty they might have had was long gone, Gordon had been of the opinion, even when he was much younger, that an older woman's face began to open in a way that he had always found more appealing than glowing skin and clear eyes. He had seen it in the faces of women standing over the copier at work, in the faces of women caressing the fresh fruit at the market, in the faces of women power walking at lunch time, along the busy streets of office buildings, arms swinging and hands curled into strong fists, heads high, their long career skirts hugging their thighs, incongruous with the running shoes tied with firm knots and loops.

Gordon had watched these faces, enjoying what he saw as a sense of freedom. These were the faces of women with children past the most troublesome ages, the acceptance of who they were and which dreams would not be accomplished and what they could still dare to hope for. He had seen these faces, and waited for the same thing to happen to Eva, to his wife of twenty-nine years.

But it didn't. Instead of opening, Eva's face began to close in upon itself. Gordon thought it took on a vague sense of melancholy, for lack of a better word. It had lost the roundness that had given Eva her youthful look; everything on her face had been round, at one time – her cheeks, her eyes, her small nose, even the edges of her teeth. Eva had not been beautiful, but seen with a certain tilt to her head, a certain distant look in her eyes, she carried a faint aura of something, some hidden longing or remorse that was surprising, and, to Gordon, quite lovely. He had once captured this look, in Newfoundland, in a photo.

Eva had been sitting on a rock at the edge of the water at Bay Bulls, her knees up and her arms wrapped around them. She had turned her face toward the water, her gaze far across the cold Atlantic, her dark hair blown out behind her, and Gordon, without her knowing, had pressed the shutter of the camera. Eva rarely spoke of her life in Hungary, but whenever Gordon saw this particular look on her face, he was certain it was a glimpse of her former life that she was reliving.

But that look disappeared, along with all the things Eva couldn't find. Her cheeks hollowed, and everything seemed to shift downward, just enough to give her a totally different appearance. It wasn't just the natural progression of time; not just the aging process. Gordon knew it was something else.

He spent a lot of time, at first, trying to find out whether what was happening to Eva was somehow related to him, to some failure on his part. The first thing he thought about was the thing most deeply buried, but, at the same time, that thing most close to the surface of their lives.

They had no children.

Eva had wanted a child almost as soon as they married, and Gordon, eight years her senior, had been, for the first few years, as eager as his wife. But after three years Eva had gone to see a doctor, and, rather quickly, it was determined that something was amiss with Eva's reproductive organs. Now Gordon suspects, from watching *Turning Point* and *Prime Time* and *W5*, that Eva's Fallopian tubes had probably been permanently scarred by some long-ago, undetected infection. But at the time that Eva had been told that she would never have a child, the doctors didn't have scans and laser microscopes and intricate testing apparatus. The doctor Eva went to seemed to be able to tell her, with certainty, that she was unable to conceive, although Gordon could never remember much in the way of explanations. He also remembers Eva taking everything the doctor told her to be gospel; it was a simpler time.

Eva once hinted to Gordon that her infertility was most likely the result of her poor nutrition in the years during the war, when she was in her adolescence. Barren was the word Eva used for herself. Along with the pattern of her speech, Eva had also used words that had an almost biblical ring.

She said it quite often, for a few years, when all their friends were producing children at an alarming rate, with seeming ease. When the people they socialized with, unaware of the pain Eva and Gordon felt, would ask questions like, 'So? When are you two going to get busy?' Or 'You two should try it.' Eva would say, lightly, but with firmness, 'Oh, we're not having children. I am barren.'

The word barren would have the effect of a heavy cloth dropped over the cage of a squawking bird; it appeared to Gordon that everyone in the room heard the word, and conversation was brought to an abrupt halt.

It had such a final ring to it. Barren. Like dead leaves, Gordon thought, their curled brown edges whispering dryly as they rushed in a pointless, swirling circle in a November wind. Like smooth grey pebbles rolling aimlessly, occasionally tumbling against each other, in the empty bed of a moving truck; like the last angry sputtering of a candle as it consumed itself in its own melted tallow.

In the moment of silence that always followed Eva's proclamation, Gordon, if sitting at a dinner table, would fold his napkin into a smaller and smaller square, focusing on lining up the corners perfectly. If standing, he would slide his hand into the right side pocket of his trousers, the pocket where he kept his loose change. Hardly moving his hand, he would concentrate on differentiating the coins, running the pads of his fingers over the Queen's head, or the shape of a caribou, a sailing vessel, a beaver. Whether standing or sitting, one thing he would not allow himself to do was clear his throat, although it ached, suddenly full of phlegm and the taste of something unknown, but bitter.

After some years Gordon and Eva's childless state wasn't mentioned any more, by their friends or by them, and Gordon and Eva concentrated on what they did best. Gordon advanced steadily in his job as an insurance adjuster, and Eva worked on turning their home into a place of beauty. Slowly, Eva educated herself about antiques, and passed on her knowledge to Gordon. Piece by piece, they embellished their home.

On their holidays, which Gordon and Eva always took on the last week of July and the first week of August, they would travel Canada, trying new foods and new wines and always finding some special item for their home. Gordon grew to look forward to these holiday pursuits as much as Eva.

The mirror had been the last thing they had bought together. It was shortly after they hung it in the hall, over the rectangular inlaid zebrawood table, that Gordon first noticed Eva's searching.

Gordon brought up the old and uncomfortable topic of their childlessness when he realized how many people their age were now talking about their grandchildren. He thought that perhaps it was this that was so distressing for Eva, the new crop of pictures of babies in the letters and Christmas cards. He thought that perhaps Eva was feeling the pain again, that it had been awakened, fresh and urgent, after all these years.

But a slightly perplexed look had come over her face as Gordon haltingly asked her, holding a Christmas card decorated with cherubs and holly, if she was having the old feelings again.

'No,' she replied. 'No, I have not been thinking about children,' and she pulled open the utensil drawer, picking up first a salad fork, and then a soup spoon. She put them both back and walked out of the kitchen, away from Gordon.

It was later that same week that he suggested they apply for a Foster Child through the 800 telephone number flashed on the bottom of the screen during one of those heartbreaking programs that seemed to dominate the television on Sunday afternoons.

Eva seemed pleased at his idea, nodding and smiling, and while she preferred that he made the phone call, she said that she wanted it to be girl, a girl of about nine or ten, one who could write back to them. She didn't care what country the child was from.

And so Gordon had phoned, and about three weeks later a large package arrived in the mail. They opened it together, as soon as Gordon had put the car in the garage after work, and looked at the thin little face staring up from the black and white snapshot.

'Bella,' Eva had read, from the form. 'Her name is Bella. From Ecuador. I would think that is a derivative of Isabelle. She is quite lovely. Look, Gordon.'

Gordon took the picture from Eva's hand. 'She's very, well, very small-looking, isn't she? For nine years old? Small, but old-looking, somehow.'

'Well, of course,' Eva said. 'She has not had proper nutrition. But look at her beautiful eyes.'

Gordon had looked back to the picture. The child's eyes were huge, and filled with something Gordon couldn't quite recognize at first. No hint of a smile touched her thin lips. Even in the uncoloured photo, the girl's lips looked cold, as if, were Bella to appear in front of them suddenly, in their bright and warm kitchen, her small lips would have a bluish cast, the kind children have after they've stayed in a swimming pool too long.

Eva had written to her right after supper. She talked about how happy they were to be her foster mother and father, and a little about their neighbourhood and the things they liked to do.

As he watched Eva read her letter out to him, Gordon pushed down the old troubling memory, the way he had refused to consider adopting a child all those years ago. It was the only thing he had ever refused Eva.

'Shall I put in a picture?' Eva said, when she finished reading.

'A picture? What kind of picture?' Gordon asked.

Eva looked at him, her eyes unblinking. 'Of us, I guess.'

'We don't have any recent ones,' Gordon said, realizing, as he said it, that he couldn't remember when they had last even used the camera.

'That is not important,' Eva said. 'Just something for her to have. To see what we are like. I will find something, maybe one of those photographs we took up at the Legislative Buildings, in Winnipeg. All the pretty flowers.'

Gordon frowned. 'That was ... that was ...' He looked at the ceiling. 'Eva, that time we stayed in Winnipeg was over fifteen years ago. We've changed so much.'

'Fifteen years?' Eva's pale eyebrows rose on her forehead. Gordon wondered when she had stopped darkening them with the little pencil she kept in the bathroom drawer. 'It cannot be that long ago. Fifteen years?' she asked again. 'Are you sure?'

'Yes,' Gordon said.

'Well, I will find something else, then,' Eva said, and left the letter on the kitchen table. Later that evening, Gordon saw that Eva had placed the letter in an envelope, a blue air-mail envelope, unsealed. He looked into the envelope, at the neatly folded letter. There was no picture.

* * *

During the first months after he'd left his job, taking an early retirement, Gordon took Eva for long drives around the city every night after supper. Eva read, out loud, all the billboards and the lit names of malls and stores as they passed. Gordon wasn't sure why she did this, but it seemed to bring her pleasure.

Eva had always loved reading, but now when he took her to the library, it distressed her. The sheer number of books and the choices involved would cause her to shake her head and pull on his sleeve, leading him toward the door, and so Gordon would leave her at home and go to the library and pick out a book that he thought she would enjoy.

He would give it to her, and urge her to sit down and read.

Then he would lower himself onto the couch and read the newspaper, glancing up, every few minutes. He would know, or at least be quite sure, that Eva was reading, because he saw her eyes move steadily along the page, from left to right, then drop, and follow the next line, and so on, until she turned the page. After ten minutes, or perhaps twenty, half an hour on a good day, Eva would gently place her book mark, a slim rectangle of brass with an E inscribed into a circle in the middle, between the open pages. She would close the book, and then carefully and thoughtfully lay it back on the Nova Scotia candle stand that served as an end table.

But then, the next time she picked it up, Gordon would see the tiny instant of panic as Eva looked at the page, then the bookmark. She would start to flip back through the pages, glancing at the bookmark, sometimes frowning, as if it, the bookmark, were the offending object, as if it had the nerve to rudely move on through the plot without her.

It took her longer and longer to finish a book, until, eventually, Gordon realized that the three-week lending time was up, and Eva was still searching for her last spot, clutching the bookmark. When Gordon took the book out of her hands and opened her fingers to remove the bookmark, he noticed that her palm, and the bookmark, were quite damp.

After that Gordon didn't take out any more books for Eva, but bought a new magazine, *Redbook* or *Maclean's* or *Country Homes*, once a week, when they did their grocery shopping. He left it on the candle stand beside the chair where Eva had always done her reading, and he was pleased when he saw that she would go to her chair, settle in it, and pick up the magazine. He watched her do this many, many times through the week. Then he noticed that each time, she would start at the front cover and work her way through to the back cover, never stopping, but turning the pages with a dull rhythm, her eyes calm and fixed on the middle of each page as it flipped past her face.

He didn't buy any new magazines after that, but left the last one on the table, and it was never mentioned.

* * *

Gordon felt a chill in the house one morning in late September, and turned on the furnace. It came on smoothly, with a little click and then a whoosh, as if it had been standing by, ready to begin its winter's work.

After lunch, while he finished drying the two soup bowls and spoons and plates and teacups, he heard Eva in the back storage room off the kitchen. There was a rustling sound, as if she were digging through layers of tissue paper.

Gordon went to get her, and found her standing in the middle of the room. The cupboard containing their Christmas ornaments was open. He shut the door, and led her through the kitchen and down the hall, toward the bedroom, for the nap she had started taking every afternoon.

'Look,' he said, letting go of Eva's arm and turning her by the shoulders, so that she faced the mirror in the hall, 'look, there, in the mirror.' He smiled at Eva's reflection. 'Do you remember when we bought this mirror, Eva? The shop in Quebec City, remember? It's a Venetian mirror, Eva,' he finished, the last sentence louder than necessary in the still house, smelling of beeswax and lemon oil.

The furnace blew a steady wave of warm air around Gordon and Eva's ankles. Gordon looked at himself, hearing a tone in his voice that was familiar, but not his own. It was the tone Eva had always used, the forced lightness that echoed with despair, all those times when she had said, 'I am barren.'

'It's the Venetian mirror you loved so much, Eva,' he repeated, his voice lower, more gentle.

Eva smiled at him, at herself, at nothing at all, at what she saw in the mirror.

After Gordon had brushed her short, thick hair and slid the sleeves of her cardigan down her arms and over her hands, and covered her with the soft wool throw he kept folded at the foot of the bed, turning the top of it down to exactly where he knew Eva liked it, just under her collarbone, he went to the hall cupboard and searched through a box.

Then he sat at the desk in the den and opened a drawer and

took out the plain manila folder.

'Dear Bella,' he wrote, on the thin blue paper, 'I am sorry to have to tell you,' Gordon paused, lifting the pen off the page, then continued, 'that all is not well with Eva.' He put down each word slowly, pressing on the point of the roller-ball pen that he felt made the best, darkest impression for the translator. 'I thought that perhaps you would like to have this picture of her, so that you would know what she was like.'

After he put the period at the end of the sentence, he set his pen beside the paper and picked up the photo, the one of Eva on the rock beside the Atlantic. He looked at it for a long time, Then, laying it on top of the unfinished letter, he walked into the shadowy hall.

He placed his fingertips, very lightly, on the configurations on the Venetian mirror, tracing their shapes. And as his fingers travelled those splashes on the surface of the mirror, he waited, waited and watched the darkening silver.

– in search of my mother's garden,
I found my own.

– Alice Walker
In Search of Our Mothers' Gardens, 1974

By My Mother's Bed

LIKE ME, Shane had grown up a Catholic; he had been an altar boy, the whole works. And also like me, he had decided to give it all up. It was strange, falling in love with someone with such a similar background. I had left my Catholicism behind with the name I had been christened – Mary Catherine – Mary Catherine of the finger-dipping, the genuflecting and whispering of imagined sins into fine mesh screens. I had tried for many years to push that girl and that part of my life from my mind.

It was actually our mutual lapsed Catholicism that drew Shane and me together. It was a Friday. The tenacity of old habits is astounding.

I moved along in the noon-hour crush at the cafeteria of my office building, automatically filling a glass with ice water, reaching for a bowl of cubed red Jell-O, then, stretching out my hand for a plate of steaming lasagna at the same time another hand reached for the lasagna immediately beside it. And just as suddenly, I pulled my hand away as the small inner voice I hated reminded me I should be taking a tuna sandwich or the seafood quiche. Because it was Friday. The other hand pulled away too. I pushed the little voice away, reminding myself, firmly, that I no longer held with such rituals, and I put my hand back out and took the lasagna, and the other hand repeated the whole bizarre comedy in harmony with mine. The curiousness of my mirrored actions made me turn and look at the person beside me, and I found myself staring into a pair of grey eyes level with mine.

'Friday fish,' the man said, then, 'or not. That is the question.'

'Not any more,' I answered.

'Me either. Not any more.'

And so we met.

* * *

Our child will be born in spring. This is good, I have been assured, over and over. I haven't figured out why this is mentioned so often by other mothers, except that spring is traditionally thought of as the time of birth and rebirth, and many creatures give birth in spring, and so perhaps this is the way nature intended it, and I'm being congratulated on this simple fact.

Shane and I have begun to think about names and are looking at wallpaper borders. I smile at him as we do these things. I also smile at the women in the express checkout at the grocery store, complete strangers, who ask me my due date. I smile at the other women who sit with dreamy expressions on their faces in the waiting room of my obstetrician. I smile and smile. I am sick at heart.

I think about this child, about who she or he will be. I think about myself, about what kind of mother I will be. And this is why I must keep smiling; so the fear that threatens to overwhelm me will be fooled, will be kept at bay.

Shane will be a good father. Of that, and only that, I have no doubt. He loves me, and will love this child that has surprised us, rather late in our lives. But then his love for me is surprising, too. I realized, with Shane, that I'd never before felt really loved. It made me feel safe, taken care of, for the first time in my life. But it also made me careless, soft, unguarded. I let happen what I swore I never would. I become pregnant. And then, of course, I was forced to do the other thing I swore I never would.

I began to think about my mother again.

* * *

I had always believed that my mother was a bad mother because she made bad choices. Once I became an adult, and could look back on my childhood and adolescence with some objectivity, I became full of contempt for her, self-righteous, even priggish. When she died, I decided that I wouldn't let her dominate my thoughts any more. I would forget all of that life, forget her. And eventually I believed I had done it. When I met Shane it had been at least ten years since I had consciously let her come back into my thoughts.

She had died at forty, two years after I left home. It was an aneurysm. Over and over, the night that Herb phoned to tell me, I pictured a sac of blood, pulsating, as the wall of the artery near her brain dilated – then the sudden explosion, a cataclysm that killed her almost instantly. Although there is no medical proof, I was sure that all the pills she took (for her nerves, she always said) had contributed to her early death. The rainbow of tablets and capsules must have had something to do with the thinning, not only of her skin and expression, but also of those veins and arteries that ran, visible at her temples, under the pale cover of her scalp. Herb told me, after the funeral, that she had been taking up to triple the medication she was supposed to, triple the pills she mentioned to me on those rare telephone conversations we had during the strained twenty-six months between my moving out and her death.

Herb sobered up after she died, and we maintained contact for a few years – mainly phone calls and one embarrassing Christmas dinner. It was in a high-priced hotel restaurant uptown, where we exchanged expensive gifts neither of us could afford or would use – I gave Herb a leather appointment book; he gave me a Hermès scarf. After the profuse thank-yous and small talk had run out, we sat in silence, cutting and chewing until Herb put down his knife and fork and lowered his face into his hands and started to weep over my mother, berating himself for not having more sense, for not trying to stop drinking sooner – that maybe if he had, he would have been able to help my mother face her demons and get off the pills and maybe she would still be alive. As he sobbed, my face burned with shame for him and for me. I wondered why I had ever imagined this Christmas dinner to be a good idea, and thought longingly of the serene silence of my small, barely furnished apartment. It was a relief for both of us when Herb moved to Parksville to take a job, and after a few letters and cards our correspondence just petered out, and there was no one left to talk to me about my mother, to make me think of her.

* * *

We learn through imitation, I have read, over and over. If this is indeed so, how did I learn to watch over my mother as tenderly as a mother watches over her own child? How did I know, at eight or nine or ten, to watch and listen for her breathing, to pull the blankets up more securely over her shoulders, to suggest she might like a bath, to try to get her to eat one of the bologna and lettuce sandwiches that made up much of my diet? Surely my case argues against the importance of imitation, and is in favour of instinct, of inborn maternal impulses. I did not learn them, for my mother showed me none, yet back then, as a girl, I possessed and acted on these instincts.

Now only a bit younger than the age of my mother when she died, I am starting to see that what I felt for her was not how a child should love its mother, but how a mother should love her child. When I learned I was pregnant, I began to ask questions of my friends who were mothers. I wanted to know about the love they felt for their children; if it had to be learned, if it was an automatic response, if it ever ran out. I didn't feel I had a single nurturing cell left. I was desperate to know if I would ever feel it again, or if I had squandered all I possessed on my mother.

One of the women I work with told me that mother-child love is binding, overwhelming, suffocating. The first time I heard these words I started at them. Bind, overwhelm, suffocate – strong words of violence and power. I thought perhaps this was one woman's experience, and that she was mistaken.

But more of my friends used these same words, went on to explain, at my expression of concern, that it is a love born of fear. At first it is fear that the infant will cry in pain and not be heard, will harbour, in its perfect new body, some monstrous disease, will stop breathing. Will die.

This initial fear passes, these same wise and experienced

friends told me, but another fills the space left by the first, possibly a little less gripping, but real fear, nevertheless. And so it goes, each stage of babyhood and childhood and adolescence passing on into the next, bringing a new fear. But it is not really a new fear. It is the same fear, surrounded by a new set of circumstances. The fear is loss, through death. And every woman said that it was the major source of fear in her life.

Over coffee with one of my best friends, Naomi, last week, I learned that Naomi's love for her children was never so strong as when they were ill. They became even more beautiful, physically, she said, during routine childhood illnesses. It was at these times, and most especially at night, that she found them unbearably radiant. As the fever would spike, predictably around midnight, the child's cheeks became flushed, the eyes, if open, dark and bright and shining, even the small lips swollen and rosy – the look of one of Michelangelo's cherubs.

And, Naomi went on, her own eyes aglow with the memory, their bodies! The warmth of the miniature torso, the fever-induced frenzied ticking of the tiny heart, causing the paper-thin skin of the chest to vibrate with its flutter. She said at times, lying beside them in bed, she would press her lips against that hot beating chest and want to drink in the little body, protectively suck it back into her own self, such was the love she felt.

And as Naomi recounted this tale of worship, the memories of my mother began to force their way back. I remembered the times I crept into her room as she slept, and crouched beside her bed, listening to the gentle rise and fall of her breathing, thanking the Holy Virgin that my mother was still alive, that I had been granted another night with her.

I was struck with the startling revelation, listening to Naomi, that I had feared my mother's death as a mother fears the death of her child. And why was I consumed by this heavy, burdened love for my mother? She gave little of herself in exchange for my open devotion; as opposed to any acts of love, my mother's message to me was one of regret, of sighs, and sad lingering looks, apologizing for having given birth to me, apologizing for her many inabilities.

This apologetic air excused my mother from being capable of helping me in any way – she couldn't be expected to know how to put the bristled rollers into my hair, how to cook even a two-course meal, how to sew a zipper into the skirt I had to make for grade eight home ec class, how to figure out algebra equations. But she was sorry! More than sorry, she was so remorseful, so penitent that my heart fairly bled to see the grief on her narrow face.

I would assure her that it was all right, it was really all right. I would try the rollers myself, again. I liked canned soup. I could ask a friend about the zipper; Sister Gilbertine, once more, about the algebra.

And her face would clear, and she would place her palm on my forehead, or the back of her hand along my cheek, briefly, as one might when feeling for a rise in temperature, and murmur, 'Good girl' and 'SUCH a good girl, Mary Catherine,' and I would feel beatified in my pain and suffering, a martyr, my glance piously lowering as I felt the hot dry touch of her hand. That I could be assuaged by so little!

After I had collected the carelessly tossed words, I would watch her slightly bowed back as she returned to the sanctity of her bedroom. There she would lie on top of her bed and sip from a heavy, finger-marked glass of milky, tepid tap water.

My mother would spend every evening resting on her bed with her water, under the mournful eyes and clasped hands of another mother, another Mary, this one hanging on the wall over the sagging double bed. Sometimes my mother would watch the evening shows, minus the volume, on the little black-and-white television on the dresser. She would stare at the screen, the harsh, jumpy patterns reflecting on her face, until she fell asleep. Then I would come in and turn off the television, remove the glass from her hand, and somehow manoeuvre her under the sheet and blankets. I would kiss her cheek, whisper, 'Sleep tight,' and tiptoe out.

After this nightly rite I would go to bed feeling mildly relieved. But I would usually wake after a few hours as if I had forgotten something important, something that nagged at the back of my mind, and I would rouse myself enough to steal back in to her room. And, like those feverish children of Naomi's, to my eyes my mother looked beautiful in the compassionate night shadows.

During the day she had a worn-out, haggard demeanour, everything about her too fine and pale, as if she were an almost transparent version of what she was meant to be. But in the darkness of her bedroom, with only the faint, fuzzy light from the lamps in the streets four floors below us, she became the mother I wanted. It was best when she was asleep on her back. In this position, her face looked fuller, more substantial, the fine etched lines at the corners of her eyes, the parentheses around her mouth all pulled smooth by gravity. Her ashen skin took on the sheen of porcelain. But it was her expression I loved the most. Serene. At peace, no longer apologetic, the lips determined, the arch of the eyebrows firm.

I wouldn't want to leave this vision. Was it because here I felt the true force of love; maybe even learned about love? Is this what was happening, by my mother's bed, in those thin hours? I grew stiff and cold kneeling there watching her in the dark. Like Naomi, I wanted to hold the thing most precious to me. I wanted to wrap my arms around her and press my body against her, make her warm, finally. But even this was beyond my grasp. Sometimes I would try to climb into bed beside her, but at the slight pressure of my body on the mattress, the whisper of cool air she must have felt on her mottled flesh as I lifted the bedclothes to slide in, she would begin to grow agitated, flinging her arms and legs about. She would gnash her teeth, and strange, undecipherable noises would emerge from deep in her throat, more than sounds, yet not words, or else words that had the texture of a foreign language, a speaking in tongues. I would listen so deeply that my neck and shoulders grew rigid, trying to figure out what it was she was saying, who she was addressing, what was so important. I think I hoped that it was me she was telling these secrets to, and by listening hard enough I would somehow figure out who this woman was, and, ultimately, who I was. And eventually, feeling worse for disturbing her solitary sleep, for causing her such anxiety by my presence in her bed, I would slink out again. Some nights were better than others – exhaustion would occasionally allow me to sleep deeply through the long dark hours. But more usually I made the short pilgrimage between our bedrooms two or three times before dawn.

Nights aside, my mother had her on days and her off days, like, I suppose, all of us. But her on days were carried out at a barely existing level, while her off days meant I was not allowed to speak to her, or make any noise. I knew immediately what kind of day it was. There was something in the air, some atmosphere, that told me how I had to act.

On those off days, I understood that it must be as if I were not there. She did not appear to notice me, unless I did what was not allowed – speak or create any noise. If I did, I seemed to bring her such unbearable pain that she would go into a kind of trance, which frightened me more than anything else I ever witnessed as a child in the sombre aridity of my home. This trance, consisting of fixed staring at some inanimate object – a picture on the wall, a dust ball under the table – was totally unnerving. She never shouted at me, or struck me, but I think I would have preferred her wrath to the unnatural shutting off that occurred if I forgot my role, if I unintentionally hummed as I opened a can of Campbell's tomato soup, or dropped a book or shut a door too loudly. And so I learned to move soundlessly, to chew with no grinding of teeth, to turn pages without even the slightest rustle, to hold in a sneeze or a cough or muffle it in a pillow.

On her good days my mother did at-home accounting. Combined with my long-dead father's small monthly pension, this work allowed us to pay for our rent and my soup and bologna and bread and her small white stapled bags from the pharmacy. And on those days, when she would allow me to speak to her, I had to address her as Mother. Such a serious term. How I longed for a Mom – actually, I longed for a Ma, like Ma Kettle, with a silly hat and a large, low bosom, someone who would diminish troubles with a Pshaw! or some such laughingly dismissive word, with a smile, or a hug.

But no. She was Mother, and I was Mary Catherine.

I wonder, now, why it took me so long to realize that Mother was in the grip of mental illness. And I wonder that no one ever wondered about me.

Did the nuns who were my teachers never think about me outside of the classroom? Did Herb, the man who came to drop off and collect Mother's work fail to notice me sitting silently on the couch when he set the pile of ledgers and papers on the coffee table and picked up the finished pile? Did the round-faced boy from the pharmacy never want to look up from the hand that placed bills into his own hand in exchange for the small white bag each week?

Obviously not. Looking back, I see now that I made myself as invisible to everyone else as I had learned to be for my mother.

* * *

As soon as I left my mother's home, a few months after I had graduated from the cool dim walls of Sacred Blood Catholic School for Girls, and had found a job and apartment, I changed my name to Kate. I liked the hard, unapologetic sound of it, the slight dare I heard in that one bold syllable.

I had escaped. Mother didn't need me around any more; she had found someone else to look after her. Somehow, discreetly, more must have passed between Mother and Herb than ledgers. One day in my second last year of high school, I came home to find Herb sitting at the kitchen table, his jacket off and his shirtsleeves rolled up. He was eating beef stew, and one of Mother's short, heavy water glasses, shimmering with amber liquid, sat in front of his plate. Mother sat across from him, an identical plate before her. There was a large pot on the stove. The counter was littered with vegetable peelings and dirty utensils. What surprised me more than finding Herb there was the beef stew. Mother had never, to my knowledge, made beef stew.

From then on Herb was around every day – there with his adding machine and supply of tall bottles when I came home from school. Mother became, for a short while, someone I didn't know. Someone who laughed and prepared simple meals, who brushed her hair and put on lipstick. Someone whose off days almost disappeared. At first I was thrilled. I didn't mind Herb being in our home; he seemed a small, silly man who drank too much, but he brought with him a secret ingredient.

The burden that was Mother was shared. My life opened up.

I joined the choir at school and stayed late for practice. I began baby-sitting regularly for Mrs Sigurdson down the hall, and for the first time had a tiny bit of money to call my own.

I felt such a rush of gratitude to Herb that one overcast spring day I even bought him a tie. I saw it in the window at Woolworth's as I trudged home from school through the slushy puddles. I'd never bought anything for a man before, and it felt somehow improper, as if I were doing something sly, underhanded. I had to will my cheeks not to flush as the cashier waited for me to dig through my wallet for the exact amount.

Herb was oddly touched by the present when I gave it to him before supper, while he was still sober. Yes, Herb seemed pleased, although I detected something on my mother's face I couldn't fathom, something that intensified my earlier feeling of guile. Her eyes rested on me in much the same way as they had all those times when I'd asked her for help, when I'd needed her to be more than she was capable of. I was filled with the old shame, as if I'd expected too much of her, as if I'd disappointed her. I told myself I'd never buy another gift for Herb.

I needn't have worried; the time for gift-giving quickly passed. Mother slipped back into her old role of sighs and stares, retreating to the bedroom earlier and earlier after supper, and staying there later and later in the morning. With

Mother's decline, the two of them no longer laughed and joked in front of the television Mother had moved out into the living room when Herb first started coming over.

Now their words were sharp, barbed, with references to people and places, to situations I'd never heard of. At times they didn't seem to be talking about the same thing, or even to each other, but nevertheless were arguing, Mother's voice muffled and accusing, Herb's slurred and defensive.

As I listened to the pitching of their words and voices, a slow, churning anxiety started to come back, grow again, deep under my rib cage. Now that Herb was seeing the real Mother, I was sure he wouldn't keep coming, would leave her, and when he did, would I have to slip back into my former role? Would I lose the first small bit of freedom I'd tasted? The hard knot of worry grew larger and larger, moving upward, threatening to choke me at times, until I felt I couldn't stand not knowing.

One Saturday afternoon, after Herb had dropped in and then gone out to pick up groceries Mother needed, I asked her, point-blank, if he would be around much longer. She looked at me, her eyebrows rising high on her still-smooth forehead, looked at me and frowned as if I had asked something bizarre.

'Around? Herb?' she said, then, 'Oh yes, Mary Catherine, yes indeed. Herb and I are getting married. I expect that as soon as you finish school you'll move out on your own. Give Herb and me the privacy we need. This apartment is too small for the three of us.'

I felt my own eyebrows lift in a parody of Mother's. It was the first time I'd heard of either issue – the marriage and my leaving. I was too stunned to question Mother further. Did she actually love Herb? Why did they fight so much, and seem so wretched, if they were planning some kind of future together? And what about me? Where was I to go? And speaking of love, did she, did Mother love me at all, that she could dismiss me so casually?

All these things whizzed through my mind at one time, and when Mother moved away from me, turned and walked slowly out the kitchen door, I just sat there, hearing through the open apartment windows the unspecified shouts of the children playing in the street below, knowing my moment for asking the questions would never come up again, that I had missed my only chance.

* * *

Shane's mother extended an invitation to me last week. Ten days away from my due date, I had started my maternity leave earlier in the month. I was finding the freedom of not working, coupled with the waiting, strangely unsettling, and so I accepted the invitation for lunch with an eagerness that surprised me.

Shane's mother said she wanted us to have some time together, just the two of us. My mother-in-law and I have nothing in common but Shane. I am grateful to her simply because Shane exists. She is grateful to me because my presence has, in a small way, brought Shane back to her. These things are unspoken between us, but known. They give us a certain liberty with each other.

We ate our lunch and afterward she gave me a gift, something the baby would need, she said, her gentle eyes, a lighter grey than Shane's, never leaving my face as I untied the ribbon and unwrapped the delicate pastel paper. I lifted out the long white lacy gown, then put it back into the box. I watched my fingers as they smoothed the tiny folds, heard something about the gown's significance, how Shane had worn it that one time, and how she had kept it all these years in the hope that it would be used again. I did thank her, but the words were weighty and dark on my tongue as I stood to leave, knowing it was impossible for me to stay any longer.

I put the box in my trunk and drove away. As I passed the park close to where Shane and I live now, I saw a few young women pushing carriages and strollers along the paths. I realized I would soon be doing the same thing, and instinctively, pulled the car over, got out and walked to a bench.

I sat there, enjoying the newness of the sun's warmth on

my face. I closed my eyes, listening to the sounds of children playing somewhere nearby and thinking about my baby and Shane's mother and the hope in her eyes. About my own mother. About what I'd felt for her those nights I'd knelt beside her bed.

And this time, instead of pushing Mary Catherine away, as I always did, I let her come. She emerged, shadowy at first, but then brighter, clearer, her face open and innocent – no, not innocent, but naïve, uncomprehending. I could see her by the bed; then, older as she sat at the table that day, hearing the children in the street below. The understanding, coming slow, that she would be able to have her own life.

And I always thought that girl had been delivered by some sheer stroke of luck, maybe by some divine hand, with Herb arriving on the scene when he did, and Mother deciding to remarry.

Sitting on that bench in the park, hearing the children's muted screeches and diluted laughter, I was able to bring back what I'd felt that day, when Mother told me I couldn't stay with her any longer. That I would have to go. I remembered my hands, clasped painfully in my lap, giving up a bit of their grip. I remembered how my stomach felt as it started to unclench, the knot that had grown so hard and tight unravelling, untying itself, and eventually, the ends floating, loose and lovely, harmless cilia letting go of their worries with wave after wave of something that I know, now, was repressed joy.

I also brought back the image of my mother, how she turned to leave me in the kitchen, and saw how her curved back held the slump not only of her usual posture, but of something else, something hard-won, and sorrowful, and yet triumphant.

And I could finally see it, could see my mother's benefaction to me, the only and most critical thing she could give. What it must have cost her.

I made my way down the narrow gravel path to my car. But before the final drive home, I retrieved the box from the trunk, and put it on the seat, beside me.

Acknowledgements

With special thanks to Randall Freeman and Carole Bernicchia-Freeman for their generous time in researching and answering questions I put to them; to Catherine Waytiuk for her helpful information; to Donna Freeman and Catherine Hunter for their reading of the manuscript, and to John Metcalf, for his patience, skill, and faith in me.

I would also like to thank the Manitoba Arts Council for their support during the writing of this book.

Several stories have appeared previously – 'Fourth of October' in the anthology *Due West*, 'Quoth the Raven' under the title 'Many Towers' in *Prairie Fire*, and 'By My Mother's Bed' in *Other Voices*.

Linda Holeman's writing covers a number of genres. Both her adult and young-adult story collections and novels have garnered national attention, and her work regularly appears in many periodicals, journals, and anthologies.

Two of her young adult novels have been selected for the prestigous Books for the Teen Age by the New York Public Library, and Holeman was a finalist for the NcNally Robinson Manitoba Book of the Year for her collection of short stories, *Flying to Yellow* (Turnstone Press, 1996).

She has travelled widely, and her past careers include a huge range – from dairy worker to a decade of teaching. She lives in Winnipeg with her husband and three children, and teaches creative writing to both adults and students.

JANZEN PHOTOGRAPHY